Blanche Willis von Teuffel

One Summer

Reprinted from the Fourteenth American Edition

Blanche Willis von Teuffel

One Summer
Reprinted from the Fourteenth American Edition

ISBN/EAN: 9783337250850

Printed in Europe, USA, Canada, Australia, Japan

Cover: Foto ©Andreas Hilbeck / pixelio.de

More available books at **www.hansebooks.com**

ONE SUMMER.

ONE SUMMER.

" Sunshine's everywhere, and summer too."

Reprinted from the Fourteenth American Edition.

TORONTO, CANADA.   SYDNEY, N.S.W.

BELFORD BROTHERS, PUBLISHERS,

MDCCCLXXVI,

PRINTED AND BOUND
BY
HUNTER, ROSE & COMPANY,
TORONTO.

ONE SUMMER.

CHAPTER I.

" The world's male chivalry has perished out,
But women are knights-errant to the last,
And if Cervantes had been greater still,
He had made his Don a Donna."
—MRS. BROWNING.

WITH a half-amused, half-impatient expression, she slowly turned from an unsuccess-
ful attempt to see through the blackness
of darkness outside the window, and looked about
the quaint old room. It was furnished with that
profound regard for angles which characterizes the
New England country-house adorned by the taste
of fifty years ago. An uncompromising sofa loftily
elevated its antique back, and contemplated with
austere approval a line of rigidly upright chairs
placed at exact distances upon the parallelograms
of the carpet, and flanked by two triangular foot-
stools. Everywhere was solidity, regularity, the
quintessence of stiffness, except in a deep recessed
window where a pretty modern Vandal, with fluffy
golden hair, was curled up upon the faded damask
cushions, and gazing with wide-open saucy eyes
upon the treasures of time surrounding her.

"Such a hopelessly heavy rain! I would like

to be a man just long enough to run down to Pratt's
for that book, but no longer; O no, not a moment
longer!" And she complacently glanced down at
the lace ruffles falling over her pretty wrists, with
conscious satisfaction shook out her soft draperies,
and meditatively eyed the tips of her delicate
French kid boots.

Renounce these delicious feminine belongings and
be transformed into a great man in an ugly tall hat
and a dress all straight lines and angles like that
odious room? Never! Not for all possible wealth
and glory and renown would she, even if it were
within her power, depart from "that state of life
into which it had pleased God to call her." It was
lovely to be a woman. She knew so many brave,
patient, noble ones. And her mind wandered to
friends far away, and, dwelling affectionately upon
their sweet and gracious womanhood, she forgot
the storm without and the prim, cheerless room,
lighted by one kerosene-lamp, which stared down
at her from the high wooden mantel like a sullen
eye gloating over the loveliness of the forlorn little
maiden. Roused from her brief reverie by

"A wind that shrieked to the window-pane,
A wind in the chimney moaning,"

she rose and slowly paced up and down the room.
The coral branches on the whatnot, the grim ma-
hogany skeleton that haunted a shadowy corner,
seemed to beckon with their white ghostly arms.
From the queer paintings on the walls, the beady
eyes of shepherdesses with brick-red feverish cheeks
watched her fixedly. "Did anybody ever really enjoy life here?" she wondered. One might drag out

a weary existence in such a place, but one could not *live.* Ah, no ! the joy of living is far removed from this desolation. Thus in the naughty impatience of youth did Miss Laura Leigh Doane dare to heap all manner of abuse upon good old Mother Jackson's " best parlour," where were arrayed her most venerated Penates, cherished objects handed down from past generations, or gathered together through the long years of her monotonous life, and always sacredly guarded from the approach of the *profanum vulgus.* The ornaments, if one may be permitted to use so frivolous a term in regard to the smaller relics, were taken up tenderly, lifted with care, when the momentous event of a yearly tea-party rendered sweeping and dusting imperative ; the more massive treasures were moved but slightly, and by the priestess's own hands, and then gently pushed back upon the identical spots in the carpet where she herself had first placed them in admiring awe half a century before. Dear old lady, who closed her eyes peacefully and was gathered to her fathers, little dreaming that ere long the sacred precincts of her " best room" would be invaded by this contemptuous young thing !

" If I could only have a grand incantation-scene, and conjure up the departed widow's wraith," the girl thought wickedly, " how I should revel in giving her a few modern ideas in regard to beautifying her homestead ! Even a ghost would be a relief to my feelings." And with a despairing sigh she drew from her pocket a letter which she had read and re-read many times since it had arrived late that day, and which at each perusal conveyed fresh aggravation to Miss Doane's perturbed spirit :

———, July 2, 18—.

MY DEAR LEIGH,—Sorry to say that some business complications have just turned up which may detain me here three weeks, and possibly longer. Bessie thought at first she would join you immediately, but dreads the long journey with nurse and baby, and so concludes to wait for me to pilot her through. You must therefore possess your soul in patience, and do try some of your winning ways on the austere Phipps, that the household wheels may run smoothly before our advent ; and above all, impress upon the worthy spinster's mind the virtue, nay the necessity of moderately late breakfasts. My six o'clock penance the morning I was there still lingers in my shuddering memory. I was not prepared to mortify the flesh so cruelly. Triumph over this abuse, my child, and you will receive my tearful blessing, and also the reward of an approving conscience, having overthrown one evil in this naughty world.

The box of books I have forwarded to-day at Bessie's suggestion. She declares you would be a miserable girl without your German and the rest of your hobbies. I saw some pamphlets down town this morning,— " Alone" and " A Waif" and " Forlorn" and " The Wanderer,"—and I ordered half a dozen to be sent up to the house, the titles were so touching and so suggestive of your situation ; so if you find them you will know whom to thank, but it is possible Bessie has scornfully rejected my humble contribution to your comfort. Do not be discouraged if the box puts in a tardy appearance in those remote wilds. Somehow I feel conscience-stricken that I left you in the forsaken old place ; but how could I deny my wilful sister when she insisted, not without reason, upon going down with me " to make things comfortable for Bessie ? " I cannot help reproaching myself that I did not bring you back ; still you are safe enough, after all, Leigh. Dragon Phipps would be a host in herself in case of anybody daring to "molest her ancient solitary reign," and I would trust that dear little head of yours the world over.

By the way, Harry Blake tells me that our old chum Philip Ogden is straying about somewhere in your vicinity in search of health and quiet. Something has given out—eyes, I believe. Perhaps you may stumble against him somewhere. I really wish you might meet him. He would make it more agreeable to you till we can get down, which you may be very sure will be just so soon as I can arrange matters. Ogden is exactly the style of man you like. If I can learn his retreat, and he is sufficiently near, I will drop him a line and tell him to call and pay his respects to the second-best little woman in the world, who is in a woful plight just now, thanks to the stupidity of her affectionate brother,

TOM.

Scrawled languidly in pencil beneath Mr. Tom Otis's dashing chirography was—

Is it not too ridiculous, you poor dear, for you to be left all alone in that horrid place ? I do not know whether to laugh or to cry, and Tom feels really dejected, though he puts on mannish airs, of course, and talks about inexorable fate, and says that you are equal to any emergency, and, moreover, that nothing so startling and unexpected as an emergency ever did or ever will happen in Edgecomb. But do be careful about fastening the doors and windows. There might be stragglers even in that innocent village, I suppose. And air our rooms from morning till night, so the sweet sunshine will conquer the mouldiness. My baby must not inhale the breath of past ages. I know you have everything ready for us even now, dear, so there's no more unpacking and arranging to occupy you unfortunately; but Tom says the place is very beautiful, which is the only consolation I have in thinking of you. You will at least have something to look at, and three weeks will come to an end sometime. But O, dear, it's so perfectly absurd for you to be there alone! I almost wish we had decided to stay at home all summer.

I'll write more when I feel a little stronger. Tom stands over me like an ogre, and threatens to take away my pencil.

Very lovingly,

BESSIE.

With a comical look of resignation the girl replaced the letter in its envelope. The situation was unpleasant, yet after all it might have been worse. The persecutions of the early Christians had unquestionably been less endurable, she thought smilingly; and then for nearer examples there was poor Robinson Crusoe, and that unfortunate young woman of Charles Reade's, whom the eccentric novelist deposits upon a lonely island with a transcendental impossible lover for her only companion. Phipps was a priceless boon compared with him. Three weeks,—only three little weeks,—not such an interminable time as it had seemed in her first disappointment when the stage-coach had lumbered along and brought the letter instead of her dear ones. And Bessie was right. The place was very beautiful. She would indeed have something to look at. Edgecomb was full of languid stately beauty, and rich with memories of days gone by, before " the vicissitudes of changeful time " had swept away its commerce and its wealth, the throbbing life from its busy marts and crowded wharves. It had a history. It was not always so silent and so staid. The city-bred girl, with her quick intuitions, had breathed in the story told by the few grand old residences, with their rows of superb and ancient elms, half unconsciously, as she had inhaled the sweetness of the new-mown hay, the heavy fragrance of the rich ripe strawberries in the fields near by, and the delicious saltness brought by the evening breeze from the not far distant sea. Even in the confusion of unpacking huge boxes, arranging their contents, and making sagacious little plans for the comfort of the invalid, Edgecomb's quiet loveliness had spoken to her deeply appreciative nature in the tender language of a benediction. The place was perfect in peace.

She would be an ingrate to rebel against her fate when she could wander about at her own sweet will, walk on that long open bridge at sunset, take a book to the summit of one of those pretty hills, and read or idly glance down on the silent river widening to the bay. Why, the prospect positively began to grow inviting. Certainly it was an unprecedented state of affairs. No one ever heard of a girl left entirely to her own devices in just this way. It was all strange. Odd that Tom had heard of the house and of its one inmate, and that his letters had prevailed upon her to move out of her accustomed grooves sufficiently to agree to take them for the summer. Such a big queer old house, and two such very queer old women had lived in it by themselves so long. The widow was a kind soul to reward her faithful Phipps—who in the good country-fashion had ministered to her as a sister rather than as a servant—by leaving her the old homestead, that she, like her mistress and friend, might die where she had lived. "Two women shall be grinding at the mill; the one shall be taken, the other left." How strange the world was! Strangest of all, it seemed to her just then that she, Laura Leigh Doane should be where she was, wondering how many cups of tea those two boon companions had drunk together. Two apiece, regularly, three times a day, not counting extras. That made twelve each day. Eighty-four a week. Three hundred and thirty-six a month. Twelve times three hundred and thirty-six?—Here she was obliged to abandon mental calculations, and resort to a pencil and the corner of an envelope. Four thousand and thirty-two in a year! And how many years? She dared not estimate. Miss Phipps's appearance would indicate a century or two. But how delightful to be in a house where for forty, fifty years at the very least, two lonely women had, amid the mildest of gossipings, solemnly swallowed every twelvemonth four thousand and thirty-two cups of tea, all scalding hot and superlatively strong! It was charming—unique, and— the lamp sputtered and the rain beat against the panes. Again she was suddenly recalled to herself. Ah, yes! everything in the world was enjoyable except that dismal room. Three weeks in Edge-comb at large, with its wealth of beautiful hills and trees and waters and invigorating salt breezes, was one thing; one evening in that room, another, altogether different and rapidly growing insupportable. She heard a step on the plank sidewalk.

She looked out, and could see nothing, but listened to the heavy tramp coming nearer and nearer. Tramp—tramp—the man had passed the window. He had been somewhere, was going somewhere. Circumstances had not conspired to imprison him in an apartment rendered hideous and sepulchral by a certain honest but mistaken widow now defunct. Thrice-happy man.

"No doubt men are blessed in some respects beyond their deserts," she said to herself, petulantly. The intricacies of politics were as Hebrew to her; she experienced no irresistible longing to be an independent voter, no mysterious magnetic drawing to the rostrum; but at that moment, which was, unknown to her, a critical one in her career, she did thoroughly covet the masculine privilege of defying storms without also defying the proprieties, and for the second time that evening came the absurd little wish to be a man for only a wee half-hour.

What would the storm and darkness be to her then? Trifling annoyances merely, not insurmountable obstacles as at present. So easy to pull on a heavy overcoat, draw a soft hat well down on the head, grasp an umbrella with one muscular hand, thrust the other in a warm pocket, and, with no petticoats fluttering in the wind and impeding progress, carelessly stalk off.

The fascinating picture suggested a certain possibility. Why should she not go out if she wished? Why might she not go down for the novel she had noticed that morning in the window of the little bookstore where she had been on some trifling

errand ?　She had wondered then how anything so
new had strayed there, and would have taken the
book, but needed no entertainment with the im-
mediate prospect of seeing Bessie and baby and
Tom.　But why should she not have it now ?　She
looked at her watch.

" Not yet half-past eight.　I'm not afraid," she
thought.　" Nothing could harm me here, and nobody knows me.　It will not take two minutes to
slip into my waterproof and rubbers.　I know I
shall not take cold.　It will be a new sensation to
be out alone in the evening, and in such a tremendous storm too.　If I meet with an adventure, all
the better.　Why it's a real Walpurgis Night.　I
shall feel like a witch."

And she looked like one as she started up with
her new resolution shining out through mischievous
eyes and oddly compressed lips.

She was young.　She had health, inexhaustible
spirits, and energy.　Her own ideas were apt to
interest her.　She was in that state of idleness in
which Satan is proverbially said to be devising
" mischief still " to cause our downfall.　And she
wanted the book.　These are the reasons, if reasons they be, why shortly after a figure, armed with
an umbrella and well wrapped in a waterproof, the
hood drawn up snugly over a close little turban,
ran lightly down the broad old-fashioned staircase,
with a gay disregard for the possible consternation
of the worthy Phipps, should she know of the wild
and wayward exploit, and gently opening the massive door, sprang with a sense of rare exhilaration
and delight out into the wind and rain.

CHAPTER II.

" 'Tis not so deep as a well nor so wide as a church-door ; but 'tis enough, 't will serve."
              —Romeo and Juliet.

ORBIDDEN fruit being ever to our fallen natures the richest and ripest and sweetest, Miss Doane experienced vivid satisfaction in executing her fantastic scheme. She hilariously floundered off and on the narrow sidewalk, always insecure, and on this memorable night rendered unusually treacherous by occasional streams of running water and deep hidden pools ; she joyously welcomed the cold rain-drops as they beat persistently against her cheek, and was intoxicated with the pleasure of struggling with all her might against the constant efforts of the wind to seize and whirl away her umbrella,—efforts which she interpreted as the playful frolics of a friend, so jovial was her mood. She skipped along, stumbled along, blew along. The mode of progression signified nothing to her. She only felt that the storm was superb, that the great elms whose swaying branches she could barely distinguish in the darkness were sobbing and sighing around her, that a mighty wind was almost lifting her bodily from the ground. She pitied girls, her former self among them, who had only ventured forth in decorous drizzles, and who knew nothing of the rapturous excitement of a mad, wild, tempestuous night like this.

She reached the bookstore, bought the coveted pamphlet. The man stared as he passed the book to her. Visions of tall girls with glowing cheeks and sparkling eyes and numerous streamlets trickling from their apparel, half-breathlessly demanding light literature at nearly nine o'clock on the stormiest of evenings, were not frequent in his limited experience, and " eyes were made for seeing." The gaze of the grim librarian did not disconcert Miss Doane in the least. She grasped her novel and umbrella, and passed out swiftly into the flood like a nineteenth-century Undine.

The buoyancy, the champagne-like frothiness of spirit still electrified her ; but, alas, champagne loses its sparkle, and forbidden fruit must some time turn to dust and ashes on the lips that taste it. As she drew near an exposed corner, it seemed as if all the winds of heaven had broken loose, were rioting madly, and seeking whom they might devour. Twice they beat her back in spite of her struggles, twitched violently at the closely fastened waterproof, and put a fiendish desire to soar away over the dusky tree-tops into her hitherto trustworthy umbrella. She retreated a step or two, stopped a moment to regain her breath, then, taking advantage of a partial cessation of hostilities, gathered herself together for a final mighty effort, and, with head bent forward, umbrella tightly clinched in both hands and held at an angle of about thirty degrees, made a grand spring, charged valiantly through the warring elements, triumphantly turned the corner, and, with singular precision of aim, plunged the apex of her umbrella directly into the face and eyes of an unwary pedestrian who was approaching from the opposite direction.

Miss Doane's momentum was great,—great also the severity of the blow she had unwittingly administered, and great the surprise and dismay she experienced at finding her freedom so suddenly brought to an inglorious end. In the confusion caused by the abrupt fall of her spirits from extreme excitement and elation to real regret, mingled with a ludicrous sense of the absurdity of her unprovoked assault, the " I beg your pardon, sir," which sprang from her heart found no utterance. After a truly feminine fashion, she ran away frantically a few feet, then stood still and speechless at a short distance from her victim.

Who was he? What was he? If it were only light enough for her to judge by his looks whether she had better offer him assistance ; for an exclamation of pain at the moment of the umbrella's direful deed, and now the stranger's motionless attitude, gave sufficient evidence that he was suffering. After all, whatever he might be, whether fierce desperado—a growth not indigenous to Edgecomb soil, she knew well—or innocent ploughboy, which was more likely to be the case, in ordinary kindness she could not leave him without a word of sympathy. Prudential motives for declining to enter into conversation with a stranger in utter darkness, and the instinctive womanly desire to be of service if she were needed; together with unusual difficulty in knowing what to say, struggled for mastery in the girl's mind during the agitating minute which followed the accident. A half-suppressed groan from the subject of her reflections made her ashamed of her silly scruples, and she moved towards him with an expression of sincerest regret upon her lips. Her remark was however unspoken, for the stranger at the same moment advanced, and in a gentlemanly voice said,—

" My good woman—"

" Good woman, indeed !" she thought indignantly and with a sudden revulsion of feeling, her sympathies giving way to wounded pride of station. " Does he take me for a milkmaid ?" Then, common sense coming to the rescue : " Well, am I not a good woman ? Naughtier than usual to-night, no doubt," with sundry misgivings as to the strict propriety of her conduct, " but a good woman, nevertheless. Certainly there is nothing offensive in the words in themselves. Nobody ever happened to call me so before, and there is a good deal in association ; but the poor man is in a dilemma, too ; how in the world is he to know in what manner to address me ?"

He evidently was somewhat embarrassed. He had hesitated after first using the obnoxious phrase ; but, reasoning that the " Madam" which would be his involuntary mode of address under other circumstances would be wholly out of place applied to a servant or to any woman out unprotected on such a furious night, he went on in a kind, reassuring tone—

" Do not be alarmed. Let me speak with you a moment."

This seemed to be an invitation to approach, as the violence of the storm rendered conversation at her present distance from him a difficult matter. There was in his manner a quiet dignity,—almost a command,—to which she found herself at once responding.

"May I trouble you to assist me ?" he asked as she drew near, and saw that he was trying to tie his handkerchief round his head, and that the wind and the necessity of holding his hat in his hand made this ordinary simple operation a difficult one. Without a word, she mechanically put her umbrella into his outstretched hand, took the fluttering hand-kerchief, folded it compactly, and tied it firmly, in accordance with his direction. "Round both eyes, if you please,—not too tight," then stood as if in a dream, awaiting further orders from this unknown and extraordinary individual. Recovering herself, she ventured to say,—

"Are you much hurt, sir ? I am very sorry."

"Not seriously, I hope, although I am in some pain," he replied. "However, it is my own fault. With such mean and miserable eyes, I ought not to have come out to-night," he continued, addressing himself rather than the supposed young rustic.

"Singular coincidence ! Neither ought I," she thought.

"My good girl,"—an indefinable something had told him that it was a young girl whose gentle dexterous hands had touched his hair,—"do you think you could—" He paused, then with some reluctance said : "The fact is, I hardly know what I'd better do. Your umbrella has nearly put out my

eye,—has injured it enough to make it exceedingly
painful, at all events,—which is not in the slightest
degree your fault, of course," he added, courteously.
" I am sorry to ask so much of any woman, particularly of a stranger ; but could you be my guide
home ? Would you object to walking to my boarding-place with me ?"

No untutored peasant-maiden could have faltered,
in reply to this somewhat astounding proposal, a
more bashful " I d-o n'-t k-n o-w" than came faintly
from the lips of the self-possessed and elegant Miss
Doane.

" These country girls are always shy," he thought,
" and no wonder she is afraid of me under the circumstances. Poor little thing ! "

Then very gently, as if encouraging a frightened
child, he explained : "Indeed, I would not trouble
you if I could help it. My eyes have been almost
powerless of late, and I hardly dare strain them by
trying to grope my way back when one eye is so
inflamed and irritated by that hostile weapon of
yours that the other is suffering in sympathy. Perhaps some man might be induced to go. The difficulty would be in finding anybody. The shops
must be closed at this hour." Then, with the
utmost courtsey : " You need not be afraid. My
name is Ogden. I am staying out at the Holbrook
Farm. Pardon me if I ask you once more if you
will be good enough to walk there with me. It is
possible for me to go alone, of course ; but difficult, and likely to be worse for me in the end—"
And he drew a long breath as if the bruise pained
him, and as if it wearied him to make so careful an

explanation for the benefit of this extremely taciturn young countrywoman.

She started when he gave her his name. She was seized with a violent impulse to seek safety in flight. "Such an incredible state of things!" she thought; then bravely accepted the situation, and said quietly,—

"I will go with you, sir."

"I thank you. Will you take my arm? I hope the extra walk will not fatigue you; yet, if you dare venture out at all to-night—" He stopped abruptly, fearing his remark might seem rude.

In her interpretation, his unspoken thought gained tenfold severity.

"A common, coarse country girl like me, who dares venture out at all to-night, cannot be injured by walking an additional mile," she thought, in much vexation. "Does he need to be formally presented to one by Mrs. Grundy, before he recognises one as a lady? Ought I to be labelled, 'This is a gentlewoman,' that the stupid man may know me when he sees me?" Then, repenting, "But the poor man has not seen me, and I have hardly opened my lips. How should he know?" After a moment she waxed indignant again. "But he ought to know. He ought to know without hearing or seeing me. I never will excuse it in him—never!"

Thus her heart full of conflicting emotions, pity for her silent companion as a fellow-creature in pain alternating with unreasoning wrath against him as Mr. Philip Ogden, who had presumed to adopt towards her a tone of calm and dignified superiority,

B

and who had not had the superhuman discernment
to recognise her, in spite of the obstacles, as his
social equal, Miss Doane walked by Mr. Ogden's
side, inwardly rebellious, outwardly guiding his
steps with praiseworthy meekness.

And, he with that sickening pain in the eyes
which sends a throbbing to the brain and intense
nervous irritability over the whole system, and
makes it difficult for the gentlest nature to be patient, thought but little of her after the brief conversation recorded. She was the means ; the speed-
iest possible arrival at Farmer Holbrook's, the end
he had in view. So through the storm these two,
whom Fate had so curiously thrown together,
pursued their way.

She knew perfectly where the farm was. She
had seen it on the main road as she entered the
village. From her lofty pinnacle on top of the
stage, she had looked admiringly upon its soft un-
dulating fields, thrifty orchards, snug cottage, and
great barns ; and Tom had inquired the owner's
name of the stage-driver, who had responded with
the eager loquacity peculiar to the genus. The
place was nearly a mile from Miss Phipps' mansion,
for whose friendly shelter she now sighed, deeming
even that much-derided parlour an unattainable
bower of bliss.

Once the idea of announcing herself to this cool
and self-sufficient gentleman, of witnessing his inevitable embarrassment should she mention her
name and Tom's, and of so revenging herself, occurred to her. But she recalled the shade of authority which she had observed in his manner, in

spite of the extreme gentleness of his tone, and also the wonder he had implied, that any decent country girl should brave the severity of so stormy a night, and unseen in the darkness she blushed crimson with mortification, and bitterly lamented her senseless whim and its consequences. She could not declare herself. She had been guilty of an act, indiscreet, according to this man's code, in the ignorant village girl for whom he had mistaken her. Should she then stop by the roadside, withdraw her hand from his arm, make a profound courtesy before his bandaged, unseeing eyes, and, after the fashion of the Sultan in the Arabian Nights, throw off her disguise, and exclaim in a melodramatic manner, "Pause, vain man! Behold in me, Miss Laura Doane, a person not entirely unknown in the polite circles in which you move, and of whom, doubtless, you have frequently heard?"

No! she was in a false position, but she had placed herself there by her own folly, and there must she remain till that fatal promenade was over.

After leaving the village, sidewalks ceased and their path lay through the muddy road. No sound was heard but the voice of the storm, until Mr. Ogden, who had apparently been forgetting his companion's very existence, said kindly,—

"I hope I am not taking you too far out of your way. This road is hard travelling in wet weather."

"It is not too far," she answered in a low voice, and with a twofold meaning of which he was unconscious. She was actually taking grim delight

in her penance. She felt that the tiresome walk
was no more than she deserved to endure. To his
mild conversational effort she responded by a brief
inquiry as to the condition of his eyes.

"Eyes are obstinate things when hurt," he said
pleasantly. "Probably I suffer more from this
evening's accident on account of their previous
weakness. There's a wretched fatality about sensitive eyes. Everything is certain to get into them,
—cinders in the cars, and umbrellas dark nights,
for instance. But I assure you they are infinitely
less painful than they would have been had I been
forced to expose them to the wind and rain, and
grope my way alone. It was the strain of trying
to keep this invalid fellow on the alert which I
dreaded, and so I ventured to trouble you. I am
very grateful to you for the relief your presence
affords me."

She knew that he must be still suffering. Evidently he would not permit the rude girl who had
caused the injury to perceive how much harm she
had done. That was generous in. him; yet he
spoiled it all by that indefinable tone in his voice.
It was not condescension,—nothing so disagreeable
as that. It was more like the over-punctiliousness
with which one remembers to thank an inferior
who does one a service. It was too careful, too
formal for equality, and it piqued her. She did
not therefore feel amiable, and she made no reply
to his acknowledgment.

They walked on in silence, and soon she saw a
light in a house which they were approaching. It
was the Holbrook cottage. All the lights were out

except this one at a chamber window. His room, she thought, as she noticed a porcelain shade softening the glare.

They reached the door of the cottage. She stopped. He quickly pushed up the bandage. "Are we here at last?" Then as he glanced up to his window, he gave a slight exclamation of pain. "I beg your pardon," he said; "the lid seems quite helpless, and an acute pain took me unawares as I looked up." She turned to go. There was a slight awkward silence; then her warm heart conquered her pride and pique.

"I am very sorry. I hope it will be better soon." She spoke in a low, constrained voice. He said,—

"Thank you. I imagine it will amount to very little." Then rapidly, as if fearing interruption, "You have done me a great service. Do not think I offer this in payment, only perhaps you know of a book or"—apparently doubting the intellectual aspirations of his guide—"a little ribbon you may fancy, and if you will buy it in remembrance of my gratitude, you will make me still more indebted to you." Putting her umbrella in her hand and with it a bank note, with a hasty good-night, he opened the door, passed in, and closed it again before the girl had recovered from the overpowering amazed indignation into which the last and most unexpected turn of affairs had plunged her.

Money! Had he dared give her money? Insulting! Incredible! She could have screamed with rage and humiliation. She never once thought of dropping it where she stood. After the first paroxysm of hurt and angry pride had passed, she held it crushed feverishly in her hand, and accepting it as the most cruel discipline she had yet undergone, the crowning torture of this wretched evening, but in no way to be escaped from, she turned from the hateful spot and started towards the village.

Her walk was sadly fatiguing. The excitement which had before sustained her and enabled her to struggle gayly with the storm was succeeded by extreme depression. The reaction had come. The rumbling of distant thunder warned her to hasten. The condition of the road, her weary feet and drenched clothing, made her progress slow. At last, as a vivid flash of lightning, accompanied by an ominous peal, illumined her path, she reached the house. The door was unfastened. The lamp still stood upon the parlour mantel. Cold, almost exhausted, enraged with herself, and bitterly denouncing the obtuseness of Mr. Philip Ogden, she wearily ascended the stairs and shut herself in her room.

She removed her wet clothing, put on a warm wrapper and slippers, let down her hair, and seated herself in a low rocking-chair for a *résumé* of the evening's woes. Her present physical comfort began to influence her views. Things did not look so utterly disgraceful as when she was wandering, forlorn and fatigued, out in the black night. Ah, but the money! How it had burned her hand all the way back! She rose and took the crumpled bill from her dressing-table. She smoothed it out with scrupulous care. She examined it with cynical interest on both sides. She turned it up and down, laid it upon her toilet-cushion, then pinned it up on the wall, and studied the effect. Two dollars Mr. Ogden had munificently bestowed upon her in token of his grateful appreciation of her services. She looked in the little mirror with a sarcastic smile that said :—" Leigh Doane, you have not lived in vain. You have turned an honest penny. You have fairly earned two dollars." What should she do with it ? Keep it for a time as a reminder of the Valley of Humiliation through which she had passed, and then drop it in the charity-box at the church door ? Yes, that would do. She laid it in her writing-desk, and sat down again to think.

A scene from one of Madame d'Arblay's novels flashed into her head. It was that thrilling moment in " Cecilia" where the adoring lover finds himself alone with his charmer in a storm. The aristocratic maiden becomes pallid, imbecile, and limp, according to the invariable custom of the heroine of the old-fashioned romance, when the slightest mental or physical exertion is demanded of her. He is nearly frantic with excess of emotion at actually being in the presence of his adored one, with no lady's-maid, companion, or stately duenna to protect her from his timorous advances. The storm increases. She trembles with fear. Her step falters. The lover observes this with exceeding solicitude, and the exigencies of the case tempting him to disregard conventional barriers, the rash impetuous youth ventures upon the unheard-of familiarity of offering his arm as a support to the gentlest and most inefficient of her sex. Aware

that the license of his conduct, though palliated by
the unprecedented circumstances, was, nevertheless, open to censure in its departure from the code
of etiquette in vogue in the painfully rarefied atmosphere of extremely high life, yet quite overcome
with the rapture of having her finger-tips resting
confidingly upon his coat sleeve, in tones of subdued ecstasy he exclaims, "Sweet, lovely burden, O,
why not thus for ever!

When this picture of the astounding difficulties
attending the course of true love in the olden time
has first presented itself to her, it had been a
source of great amusement. Indeed, many novels,
dear, no doubt, to her grandmother, were wont
to convulse her with irreverent mirth. Could
anything be funnier than the stilted phraseology of
those love-sick, perplexed swains, and the laments
of lachrymose heroines who wring their hands frantically on all occasions, and evince a chronic incapacity for doing anything of the least use to any
human being? She had sometimes congratulated
herself upon being commonplace Leigh Doane in
the present state of society, instead of a Sophronia
Belinda Araminta Clarissa Mac Ferguson under the
old régime. But never had the contrast between
then and now, between the lifeless but highly decorous demeanour of the model girl of the past
"period" and the extravagant wilfulness of her own
conduct, struck her so forcibly. Madame d'Arblay's
representation of maidenly propriety, the ever-
lovely Miss Beverly," had nearly fainted in the
fiery ordeal of walking a short distance with an
esteemed gentleman friend in broad daylight. She,

on the contrary, a girl most carefully reared according to modern ideas, had manifested sufficient discreditable vigour to nearly annihilate an unknown man, and had then walked by his side and guided his steps over a long, rough country-road, in intense darkness and a violent storm. She remembered mild, timid, clinging Cecilia, and smiled. She thought of fearless, self-confident Leigh, and groaned.

Now, if he had only thrust an umbrella into her eye, how much better it would have been! It is woman's province to suffer, and it would have been the most natural thing in the world for her to meet with an accident ; quite romantic had she been obliged to accept the escort of an unknown gentleman, who would eloquently protest that he never could forgive himself for his awkwardness, and who would prove to be Tom's old friend. But how unnatural, how ridiculous, for her to savagely charge at him, and then in silence, like a bashful, stupid rustic, take the wounded man to his destination! The former case would have been like some piquant little adventure in a book. As it actually happened, it was grotesquely transposed, and all wrong. What would Bessie say? Tom should never know. He would tease her too unmercifully. And as for his friend, Mr. Ogden, whose mental vision must be as blind as were his outward eyes, she would never, never meet him if she could help herself, and she would despise him, upon principle, all her life. " My good girl—" Here an overwhelming consciousness of the utter ludicrousness of the affair from beginning to end rushed over her, and she laughed aloud.

Peal after peal of nervous hysterical laughter burst from her lips, until the tears rolled down her cheeks. Luckily Miss Phipps was too remote to be roused by this untimely merriment, or she would have risen in alarm, fearing for the sanity of her young guest. The ebullition proved a relief. It carried away much self-reproach and chagrin from the girl's mind. It left regret and some humiliation, but also the more cheerful tendency to look upon Mr. Ogden's uncalled-for generosity as an enormous joke rather than as the personal insult she had been inclined to consider it, and she laid her head on her pillow more happily than she would have deemed possible an hour before. But immutability is not a characteristic of one's emotion at twenty. Her experience that evening had been a varied one, and she had passed through a thousand phases of feeling.

Her last thought as she closed her eyes was, " ' Perhaps you may stumble against him somewhere,'—O you wise, prophetic Tom ! "

CHAPTER III.

"He would have passed a pleasant life of it in despite of the Devil and all his works, if his path had not been crossed by a being that causes more perplexity to mortal man than ghosts, goblins, and the whole race of witches put together, and that was —a woman."— WASHINGTON IRVING.

THERE are eyes and eyes. Popular prejudice leans towards fine eyes in works of fiction, but as a faithful historian this chronicler must dispassionately state that Philip Ogden's were not such as should appertain to the hero of a love-story. They did not glare fiercely from beneath shaggy brows, like those marvellous deep-set gray ones of a certain school of romance, nor were they in the habit of assuming a cold and inscrutable expression to the world at large, and then " melting dangerously," whatever that may mean, for the especial delectation of one favoured mortal ; neither could they flash, nor burn, nor frighten people with a steady ominous glow, nor, in short, execute any feats of a pyrotechnic nature. At their best, viewed in the friendliest light, they were ordinary blue eyes, with a sufficiently sensible and agreeable expression, in which, perhaps, lurked a remote suggestion that Mr. Ogden might not need to have the point of a joke explained to him. It may also be said that they were extremely near-sighted, and apt to feel weary and overworked unless used with care. As they were not likely to recover easily from violent shocks, it is evident that Miss Doane's umbrella made an injudicious selection of a victim. In this opinion, Mr. Ogden would no doubt have fully concurred.

The fair summer morning stole into his room and found him sleeping in serene unconsciousness of coast-storms, pugnacious girls with umbrellas, his disfigured countenance, and all sublunary ills. But the crowing, and quacking and lowing, and the other noises whose distant echoes sound so sweetly in pastoral poems, and "voices of men and voices of maids," and more especially the far-re-sounding twang of the mistress of the farm mus-tering her forces, conspired to rouse him at an early hour from his blissful ignorance. With the aid of a hand-mirror and his one available eye, he exam-ined the puffed-out, angry-looking cheek and swol-len, closed lid which marked the ravages of the destroyer.

"That was a fell swoop, but the blow was ad-mirably aimed. If you had struck higher you would have put out my eye ; lower, you would have loosened a few teeth. You punched better than you knew, my fair Phyllis."

He carefully closed every blind and drew every curtain, shutting out the "jocund day," whose ever-increasing radiance he had no eyes to see ; and, like a boy afraid of ghosts, who whistles in the dark to keep up his courage, he hummed the cheerful and appropriate ditty,

> " There was a man in our town,
> And he was wondrous wise ;
> He jumped into a bramble-bush,
> And scratched out both his eyes,"

as he renewed his bandages and placed a bottle of arnica—which he regarded as his only friend—at a convenient distance from the sofa, upon which he finally threw himself, painfully aware that he was a doomed man for that day, and for how much longer he knew not.

"Time and arnica make a powerful combination, and will heal my woes as they have healed worse ones before now. 'From him who hath not shall be taken away even that which he hath.' 'Grin and bear it,' is sound philosophy, and is, after all, only Epictetus condensed. Grin, I may. Bear it, I must. Upon the whole, I think I will grin." And something of the nature of a smile played about his distorted features, giving him a sardonic and unamiable aspect of which he was quite unconscious, and quickly followed by a very unphilosophical yawn and sigh. The circumstances were not conducive to philosophy, and the young man did not feel like a hero. Things looked uncommonly doleful. He was not sublime. He was not pathetic. He was simply ridiculous, and he knew it. It occurred to him that not one of the grand old philosophers could have posed much for future generations, situated as he was. "Philosophy is a delusion and a snare," he thought. "It is easier to write sage truths and be stoical on paper, than to evince much grandeur of spirit lying in a dressing-gown and slippers on a hard sofa in a commonplace farm-house, with an aching head and a black eye. Now, I might summon Jimmie up here, and, folding my toga solemnly about me, show him 'how sublime a thing it is to suffer and be strong,' but Jim has not that meek and lowly spirit which is an ornament to youth. I fancy my visage might excite unseemly mirth in the little rascal, and moral maxims, issuing from arnica bandages, would be apt to lose their potency. How in the name of all that is wonderful did the girl manage to do so much mischief without doing more ?" he asked himself. "If that umbrella—may the foul fiend fly away with it !—had had a pointed end—" Why, how did the thing end? It was a small, light, a lady's umbrella. Where his hand had rested, there was a cross. He now remembered feeling the horizontal piece of metal,—was it not? It all came back to him plainly. A pretty little umbrella, probably, with a silver cross on it, perhaps, and some sort of ornament on the other end,—which was, thank Heaven, blunt!—in short, an umbrella such as city girls carry. Odd for this girl to have such elegant ·belongings. Yet life is an enigma. Jane Maria Holbrook went to the pasture "to call the cattle home" with a black lace mask veil strapped tight over her sharp nose. She too, poor child, has aspirations !

At this moment Jane Maria knocked and giggled at the door. It is perhaps superfluous to say she giggled. She knocked, is sufficient. The giggle accompanied and followed every act and speech of the ingenuous Jane Maria. She was nineteen, and she read the New York *Ledger.* Mr. Ogden was not an Adonis, under the most favourable circumstances : but Jane Maria thought him " perfickly splendid," he was so much like Lord Romaine Cecil Beresford in the "Haunted Homes of Hills-

dale ; or, The Thrilling Three." Mr. Ogden told
her to come in, and the girl ventured to open the
door, then stood in real distress to see the man so
like her favourite hero in the " H. H. of H.," etc.,
lying on a sofa with a ghastly white handkerchief
spread over his aristocratic features, and revealing
to her troubled gaze only a portion of that noble
brow which was the counterpart of Lord R. C. B.'s
in the electrifying romance before mentioned. Mr.
Ogden spoke in his usual tone, thereby dissipating
any vague fears that he had been cruelly wounded
by base ruffians while wending his way over the
gloomy heath.

" Miss Jennie, I ran against something last night,
and hurt my eye a little. Please tell your mother
I do not wish any breakfast, and that I have everything I need."

Jane Maria was a silly child, no doubt, but she
had a good heart, and she was very sorry to see
Lord Romaine, that is, Mr. Ogden, in so helpless a
condition, and she did not believe he was comfortable, and she stood swinging the door and agitating
her elbows and blushing violently ; all of which
Mr. Ogden knew quite as well as if his eyes had
been wide open and fastened upon her. He did
not know, however, that her very soul overflowed
with gratitude every time he addressed her as
" Miss Jennie," a kindly softening of the detested
Jane Maria which he had chanced upon only because " Miss Holbrook " failed, he had discovered,
to distinguish the daughter from the mother.

"If there is anything I could do, Mr.—— " she
faltered, almost saying Beresford, and, in her confusion, not daring to attempt Ogden.

"Nothing, thank you, Miss Jennie, unless" — feeling her disappointment—"you would have the kindness to bring me some fresh water."

She left him and soon returned with the water and the maternal Holbrook, who came up with the evident intention of staying an hour or two and learning all the particulars of the accident. It required the exercise of much tact and irresistible gentleness of manner, which was perhaps his peculiar charm, to undermine the curiosity of his hostess and baffle her cross-questioning without giving offence, and to plead a nervous headache and increased inflammation of his eye if he were not left in perfect quiet. He knew enough of Edgecomb ways to feel tolerably certain that a plain statement of the facts of the case would be more than sufficient to cause the circulation of marvellous fables in which perhaps would figure a legion of young Amazons armed with gigantic umbrellas, and there would be nothing whatever left of him. Mrs. Holbrook went down to her household cares hardly realizing, until her departure, that she had gained no information concerning Mr. Ogden's affairs, and then formed a theory of her own, that her "city young man" had fallen down and hurt himself, and was ashamed to tell of it, which wise conclusion she boldly advanced as an historical fact; while poor little freckled Jane Maria went about in a dream all day, and looked upon Lord Ro— Mr. Ogden's accident as a beautiful mystery into which she could not and would not penetrate.

As for the young man himself, he enjoyed the encounter, but was thankful that it was brief, and, as Mrs. Holbrook finally twanged out her adieus and left him weak yet victorious, he applied his arnica and water with a placid smile, and thought that after all there were evils in life worse than a bruised eye and solitude. Yet the woman meant well. She was shrewd enough too. Considerable strategic ability was necessary to turn her questions out of their course without letting her see what he was doing. "She probably could assist with cool nerve and steady hand at the amputation of a man's leg, but what does she know of the æsthetics of a sick room? She would drive one into a nervous fever, with her questions, her diabolical voice, and her heavy step. And Jane Maria, too, poor girl, how she giggles, and rattles the door-knobs, and works those elbows!" Thus he mused more in sorrow than in anger. He had supposed there were some things which all women knew by intuition. That refinement, training, were non-essentials in a sick-room; that the womanly heart was the one thing needful. Well, it was only another lost illusion. Holbrook, *mère*, might have a womanly heart. He certainly knew nothing to the contrary. But she could never be anything but elephantine. He was inclined to believe too that little Jennie could never learn to pour water without deluging everything; still, she was young and might admit of reform.

Through the long day he lay dozing, thinking, smoking, listening to the busy sounds from below, occasionally pacing up and down his room, but returning gladly enough to his couch, finding more relief there than elsewhere. He was a man who

C

knew little of what he had called the æsthetics of
a sick-room, except from vague recollections of his
childhood and from theory ; but, falling towards the
close of the day into a mildly sentimental reverie,
he fancied that it might be an agreeable sensation
to have soft hands quietly, and unsolicited, mois-
ten his bandage when the fever in his face heated
it ; that a favourite poem or attractive essay, read
with the sweet and appreciative intonation which
would unquestionably be a special charm of that
"not impossible she," would not only be an indescribable relief to the monotony of such a day,
but a blessing for which he thought he should know
how to be sufficiently grateful. Yes, his ideal
woman should have all the graces of the art of
ministering. Her boots would never creak. Her
dress would never rustle. She would not annoy
him with a perennial giggle, nor shake the rafters
with her massive tread. She would, in short, he
concluded, disgusted with his own poor perform-
ance of the rôle of sister of mercy, be a perfect
woman nobly planned to administer cool bandages
with skill and dispatch, and without sending rivu-
lets to penetrate his left ear, as he was then doing.
How would the mingled fumes of arnica and an
unlimited number of cigars impress this paragon
whom he was in imagination introducing into his
apartment, he wondered, as he ventured, now that
the sun had almost set, to throw open the blinds
of an east window. She would manage in some
way to make things pleasanter, no doubt. Girls
knew how, he supposed. She might sprinkle eau-
de-cologne on his pillow and about the room, per-

haps. A man would not think of coddling himself, but he was not sure that he might not like that sort of thing well enough if it were done for him, he admitted with that gracious condescension men sometimes evince towards ways essentially feminine. At all events he could testify that the room was unpleasantly close, and the smell of arnica inhaled steadily for more than a dozen hours an unmitigated bore. Where was it lately he had noticed an especially delicate perfume? Not last night, was it? Ah, yes! He recalled the circumstance now. It was when that shy damsel was tying the handkerchief for him, and again as he stood near her a moment down at the door. He reflected smilingly, that he had felt savage, infuriated like any other wounded animal he supposed, consequently in no mood to appreciate perfumes, were they wafted from Araby the Blest, or to speculate upon evidences of refinement in an Edgecomb belle; but it struck him now, lying smoking and musing at his leisure, as singularly incongruous that she should fancy a faint, delicious odour. Now, if it had been musk,—double extract of musk,—Jane Maria would like that, he was sure. Was it violet? Of that he could not be quite certain. But whether it floated from her hair, from glove or ribbon, something dainty and lady-like there had been, he was positive. And—starting up suddenly—was he a fool that he had not thought of it before?—she walked like a lady. He had escorted Jane Maria to "meetin'" one evening. She had taken his arm as if it were a remote and dreaded contingency. This girl, on the contrary, had accepted it as an arm simply, and

leaning slightly upon it, had moved in spite of wind
and rain, and the poor condition of the road, with
the elasticity and firmness of a person whose feet
are used to city pavements, and whose mind is used
to the friction of city life.   Her gait was a forcible
contrast to the slow, heavy, aimless step, prevalent,
he had observed with surprise, in Edgecomb.   For
where should one look for health and energy, if not
among country girls ? he wonderingly asked himself.   Yet the rapid, vigorous step, the fresh colour
which he would have frequent occasion to admire, a
cool, clear day, on any pleasant avenue in a city, he
had not once seen in this breezy village, where the
air was so pure and invigorating it was almost
enough to make the lame walk.   To which class,
then, did she belong, this mysterious escort with the
erect, spirited carriage, the mystical, faint fragrance,
the gloved hands, the elegant though vicious umbrella, and the *accent,*—yes, unquestionably, the
accent of a lady ?   Although her words were few,
any man not an egregious dolt would have observed,
in spite of personal discomfort, her manner of
speaking.   How, then, did she happen to be out ?
That was not his affair, certainly.   She must have
thought his coolness satanic.   Gave her some money
too ! H'm !   And he lay back on his sofa in mute,
inglorious despair, for the consciousness that the
girl was a lady had burst upon him like a revelation, with overwhelming force.   He could not doubt
it.   His conviction now was as strong as his utter
obliviousness had been before.   He muttered a few
energetic imprecations upon his selfish stupidity,
but was nevertheless intensely amused at the unconscionable aspect of affairs.

A woman ! A woman, of course, or all would yet be well ! A man would have defined his position at once in some way. A man would have declined taking the extra walk, or he would have taken it as a friend in need, or he would have gone with the hope of reward, had he belonged to the class that pockets fees. In either event there would be no more trouble. But now ! No more free enjoyment of the lavish summer for him ! No more lying about lazily, yet with a clear conscience, feeling that it is " enough for " him "that the leaves are green," and "that skies are clear and grass is growing." Ah, what a huge humble pie it would soon be his doom to swallow !

I must find her and ask her pardon on my knees ; but what is an apology, after dragging her a couple of miles and paying her like a coachman ? My mission in Edgecomb is revealed, at all events. Fortunately, in this communicative hamlet, it will not be difficult to ascertain who she is and where she is staying. "It is curious," he said aloud, and with great deliberation and emphasis, "how completely a man will sometimes stultify himself ! Blind, imbecile coxcomb ! "

CHAPTER IV.

"The prudent penning of a letter."

EDGECOMB, Friday, July 6, 18— .

SWEETEST, my sister, was it for this I toiled
and suffered? Was it for this I turned Miss
Phipps's theories and rooms topsy-turvy, and
hammered my fingers, and tore the trimming off my
sleeve? The talent I have displayed as an upholsterer
and general decorator is surprising, and my acrobatic
feats, if I may so classify balancing myself upon chair-
backs and certain inevitable results which might reasonably be called "lofty tumbling," truly admirable in an
inexperienced performer. And if you could have the
faintest idea of what I have been able to accomplish
with that commonplace and insignificant thing, an
umbrella, you and Tom would be perfectly amazed.
But, as the books say, "we anticipate."

Bessie, it grieves me to the heart to think that before
you come the first bloom will have vanished from my
triumph of art, the great high-backed chair upon which
I have nearly exhausted my genius and my chintz.
Yesterday afternoon I drew it up to a window where
one looks out on a charming little picture framed by
the branches of two beautiful elms that stand near the
house,—the pretty, sloping common, and old, old sun-
dial in its centre, and its other edge bordered by elms,
and behind them a row of quaint cottages, beyond, a
glimpse of the river, and still beyond, the hills, with
their lovely, changing lights. In a few moments you
would be there. Everything did look so pretty, Bessie.

I turned on the threshhold to give a parting glance into your room before I went down to the door to wait for the stage. A light breeze just rustled the fresh chintz curtains, gently shaking their pretty, pale blue morning-glories and humming-birds, and carried through the room a faint fragrance of mignonette and pansies, and there was the dear old chair waiting to receive you, and looking positively expectant. It really has a great deal of expression, and it had such an inviting, hospitable air, such a benevolent and expansive smile, that I had to give it a little pat of approval every time I went near it. Everything was ready, and I was so happy, and was fancying how delightful it would be to usher you up to your nest, and, pointing to the curtains and toilet-table and the various things I had prepared for your comfort and pleasure, modestly, yet with pardonable pride, say, "These are my jewels." Just then I heard the stage. Out of the house I "flung,"—why may I not say it if Robert Browning does?—I stood at the gate and watched that ancient vehicle toil up the hill. Imagine my distracted state of mind when it actually went lumbering by. I could not believe my eyes. No, Bessie, no baby, no Tom! Like that pathetic "dove on the mast as we sailed fast," I did "mourn, and mourn, and mourn." With a desolate, moated-grange sensation, I turned and went into the house. At the door stood Miss Phipps, eyeing me curiously.

"Oh! yer folks didn't arrive, did they? Oh!"

I replied with some dignity, and a huge lump in my throat, that something apparently had detained my friends. I passed up-stairs. What a change in those few moments! The sky had grown cloudy. The breeze was chilly and damp. The distant hills looked cold and gray. The curtains suggested the vanity of all human hopes. The chair stood a great clumsy, melancholy monument to the transitory nature of happiness.

For an individual who has always professed to doubt the efficacy of tears, I had a singularly strong inclination to cry. The disappointment was so sudden, so bewildering, you see. I could not stay up there. I grew too homesick. I closed the windows and door and wandered about drearily, and then I sat down in the porch, watching the clouds gathering fast, and waited there "exceeding comfortless" until a small boy for whose trustworthiness Miss Phipps vouches, and whom I have engaged to bring my letters, appeared with Tom's document, and I learned my fate. Mr. Mercury, otherwise Jimmie Holbrook, seated himself on the fence, whistled "Shoo Fly," swung his feet vigorously, and stared at me intently as I opened my letter. I glanced up, and said solemnly,—

"That will do, James. I do not want you any longer."

Could any one have received a more direct dismissal? You imagine that he at once retreated respectfully from the presence, do you?

On the contrary, he smiled in an imperturbable manner, and responded cheerfully,—

"Well, you ain't likely to have me any shorter. Fences is free, and I like yer looks!"

This astounding declaration silenced me. Reflecting that Jimmie probably had not a judicious mamma, and feeling rather grateful to the child for diverting me in my sadness by his good-humoured impudence, I read and re-read Tom's letter and yours, and meditated gloomily until the "silent mist came up and hid the land," and the air grew more damp and more salt every moment, and finally down came the rain. Down also came that terrible child from his post of observation. He responded to my "Good night, Jimmie," with singularly explosive shrieks and uncouth pirouettes, and started off in a rapid and impish manner for his home. And I went in to my lonely supper, a cold, forlorn, homesick, wretched girl.

And afterwards—O Bessie, I *could* a tale unfold. But I will not, because you have a Tom who hears all your secrets. If I disgrace the family while I stay here, remember it will be his fault, for he left me. Do not be alarmed. Phipps and I have not come to blows yet, though what may result from my sojourn remains to be seen. I have certainly developed some hitherto latent traits, or " tricks and hammers," perhaps I should say, and it is impossible to tell where I shall stop. There is a room here that is positively maddening if you stay in it long enough, and there are electrical currents in the Edgecomb atmosphere that make " gleams and glooms " dart across one's brain in an inexplicable way, and my conduct has been most strikingly original— wherein lies a pointed joke, and yet no joke.

As you must see, there is a burden on my conscience. I shall never rest until I make my confession. But not to-day. It is too soon, and then, there's Tom.

It is a glorious morning. You will enjoy the air here so much, and the views, which are charming in every direction. I am going out directly to mail my volumin- ous letter, and to discover the pleasantest walks in this pretty neighbourhood. I have resolved to be as cheer- ful as circumstances will permit. I am not yet "recon- ciled," but have recovered from the first crushing effects of my grief. I am " beginning to take notice," as some one said about our friend the pretty widow. Something has partly turned my attention from my disappointment, and set my thoughts running in cu- rious channels. My secret is on the tip of my pen, and dying to drop off. To-morrow, perhaps I will disclose my guilt in its enormity. Bessie, of course I have done nothing darkly and desperately wicked, but do come quickly. I am not so reliable as I thought I was. Tom's confidence in what he is pleased to call my "clear little head " is sadly misplaced. Everybody has been mis- taken in me always.

Have I told you what a furious storm there was last

night? It made a greater impression on me than ever a storm did before, and I am not the only person in Edgecomb who has reason to remember it.

Grow strong very, very fast, kiss baby for me, and make Tom bring you soon to Edgecomb, and

Your loving

LEIGH.

Accompanying this epistle was the following :—

Thanks for your letter, my dear Tom, and I may eventually thank you for allowing your "business complications" to detain you, but I must confess I do not feel grateful yet. There is, I suppose, a law of compensation, and no loss without some gain, they say, and Edgecomb may have something beautiful in store for me, but it has not begun well. Do hurry, Tom; that's a dear boy. Never mind business. And, Tom, you need not give yourself the trouble to hunt up that friend of yours, that Mr. Ogden, and send him to call upon me. I do not think I would like him. I know I should not. I am convinced he is "exactly the style of man" I always heartily dislike. Please don't, Tom!

CHAPTER V.

" You lazy, not very clean, good-for-nothing, sensible boy ! "—
THACKERAY.

THE umbrella catastrophe enforced upon Mr.
Ogden a week's seclusion, in which the stupidity of one day differed but slightly from
the stupidity of another.   An avalanche of questions from Mrs. Holbrook, concerning the smallest.
details of his previous history, as well as his intentions for the future, threatened daily to overwhelm
him, but, thanks to his mental agility, he escaped.
He gradually learned to consider each contest with
her a matutinal tonic, unpleasant but strengthen-
ing.   Before her advent he fortified himself.   He
studied an unsatisfactory and mystifying style of
conversation.   He intrenched himself behind the
longest words in his vocabulary, and when they
failed he did not hesitate to coin longer ones.   The
subterfuges to which he resorted in order to
shorten her visits were invented with rapidity and
ease, and displayed a neatness of execution upon
which he congratulated himself, being but a novice
in the art of finessing.

Upon one occasion, when Mrs. Holbrook entered
his room, she found him lying with a handkerchief
over his face, his hands clasped peacefully on his

breast, while his gentle, regular respiration, placid as that of a sleeping infant, pleaded eloquently in his behalf. Her step became no lighter, her voice no less harsh and discordant out of consideration for the invalid's nap, and Jane Maria as usual convulsively played her Rondo Capriccioso upon the door knob, but nothing apparently could disturb that beautiful repose. Though this artifice routed the enemy, Mr. Ogden felt that a repetition of it might create suspicion in the least astute mind, since Mrs. Holbrook's colossal presence would have awakened the Seven Sleepers; " and then," he thought, " a man who from the nature of his position idly dozes through a good deal of the day, and who has openly confessed to his tormentors that he habitually sleeps well nights, cannot reasonably be at it again at eight o'clock in the morning. There's a limit to all things." He forebore, and developed other resources.

Once he greeted her with rambling, incoherent words and confused utterance. He endeavoured to arrive at a golden mean between delirium and idiocy. In this temporary derangement of the intellect, he did not aim at wildness that would alarm her, and cause her to summon her husband and the labourers, the long sweep of whose scythes he could hear near the house. Hopeless, impenetrable dulness, absolute incapacity to receive or impart ideas, was his artistic design. This he at first regarded as magnificent strategy, and decidedly his best effort, but modified his views when, to his horror, she came again that day. His faculties were so benumbed by her unexpected appearance, that, had she but appreciated her advantage and pursued it skilfully, it is probable that he would have told her everything he knew. He blessed the unknown voice which called her down to her own domain, and realizing that this time fate, and not, as before, his own exertions, had extricated him from his danger, consoled himself with the reflection that there must be one unguarded moment in the life of the craftiest diplomatist.

These trials of skill were somewhat enlivening. He also derived a mild excitement from observing the new and startling hues which the variegated cheek assumed as his swollen face gradually regained its natural outline, and the endangered eye feebly yet gladly beheld again the light of day.

Jane Maria blissfully served her wounded knight's repasts, and evinced a sincere though tremulous desire to do all in her power for his comfort. One morning, when she inquired, as usual, if he wished anything more, he abandoned his formula, " Nothing, thank you, Miss Jennie," and surprised her by saying he thought he should enjoy a call from Jim, if the boy did not object. Why any person, not forced to submit to the infliction of her mischievous brother's presence, should deliberately seek it, was beyond her comprehension ; but Mr. Ogden's slightest wish was law to this adoring soul, and inwardly responding, " I fly, my lord, to execute thy mandate," she went to find Jimmie.

Some time elapsed before he appeared. He had first to be discovered. This the loyal Jane accomplished after a vigorous search in his most

frequented haunts, and Jimmie was torn with a
ruthless hand from the innocent pastime of trying
to induce two superannuated roosters to pick out
each other's eyes, and was half dragged, half coaxed
into the house. Here Jane Maria resigned the
command, and the child, thanks to his mother's
efficient generalship, after a sound of scuffling at
the foot of the stairs and other indications of a
family jar, finally presented himself before Mr.
Ogden.

It was evident that the prospect of a *tête-à-tête*
with the invalid, in what he had a moment before
distinctly and turbulently called "that darn poky
old room," was not alluring to Jimmie.

Mr. Ogden appreciated the boy's feelings, and
did not wonder at the somewhat morose aspect of
his young visitor.

"Ah, Jimmy, is that you? How are you to-
day?"

"Well enough," was the brief response.

"Sit down, won't you?"

"Can't stop. Ain't got time," the child replied,
with an uncompromising air. His terse style of
conversation was a refreshing contrast to Mrs. Holbrook's volubility. Mr. Ogden had certain profound reasons for desiring to propitiate Jimmie.
Ignoring the boy's dogged manner, he said carelessly,—

"Any candy-shops in Edgecomb?"

"Rather!" Jimmie replied with emphasis.

"Jim, do you like taffy?" was the next signifi-
cant inquiry.

"You bet!"

Here a silent transfer occurred.

Jimmie pocketed the "filthy palimpsest" with a very slight increase of cheerfulness. His was not one of those base natures with which money is all powerful. He still sighed for his freedom, for his roosters. He was mollified, not completely subdued. Mr. Ogden, observing this, played his highest trump. Removing the damp cloth which he still wore upon his face, he said,—

"What do you think of that for a black eye, Jimmie?"

Liveliest interest was instantly depicted on the child's countenance, as he eagerly asked.—

"Who did yer fight? Did yer lick him?"

Here was a dilemma. But Mr. Ogden could not afford to lose the point he had gained. With Machiavellian policy, he solemnly remarked,—

"Jimmie, I always lick when I fight."

"Do yer, though? Honest? Let's feel yer muscle."

With much inward amusement, but with a perfectly grave face, Mr. Ogden submitted his arm to the critical examination of his young visitor, who manipulated his biceps with the air of a connoisseur, and admiringly expressed unqualified approval.

"Reggler stunners, ain't they?"

Jimmie was won.

From that moment he was

> "Rapt
> By all the sweet and sudden passion of youth
> Towards greatness in its elder,"

and looked upon Mr. Ogden as Lavine upon Launcelot with that

> "Reverence,
> Dearer to true young hearts than their own praise,"

or to descend abruptly from Tennysonian heights
to Jimmie's level, and use a comparison within his
grasp, Mr. Ogden became as glorious in his eyes as
a champion prize-fighter, and the boy went freely
in and out of the room during the two remaining
days of the captivity with the glad conviction
that he had found something more precious than
roosters.

"Mr. Ogden promised to tell Jimmie some time
how he had received the bruise. Just now he
wished "nothing said about it." Jimmie gave a
knowing wink, and unhesitatingly swore secrecy.

Then, not only to advance his own interests, because Jimmie himself was a safer person to cate-
chise than any of Jimmie's kinsfolk, but because
he found the child's bright face and sturdy, honest
ways attractive, Mr. Ogden became fascinating in
the extreme, by asking about trout streams, and
how far out they had to go for mackerel, and by
talking of wherries, of the impending circus, of
birds' eggs, and finally he approached the important and long-delayed topic.

"Are there many strangers in Edgecomb this
summer, Jimmie ?"

"Well, there's you," said the boy, " and there's
some folks down to the tavern, and there's *my*
girl, and that's about all there is there now, I guess.
Sometimes there's more."

"And who might your girl be ?"

"Why, the one I take letters to," said Jim, drawing himself up with dignity. "She gits a heap.
She's had four, and she aint been here two weeks
yet."

" Then you know her name, of course ? "

" Once it was Miss L. L. Doane, and twice it was Miss Doane, and the last time it was Miss Laura Leigh Doane."

" Doane—Doane," thought Mr. Ogden ; " who was it married a Miss Doane while I was abroad ? If I am not mistaken, it was Otis. But it may not be the same family. Nor Jim's young lady, my young lady."

Jimmie went on—

" She's to ole Miss Phippses, yer know. Her folks was a-comin', but they ain't come yet. She's mighty anxious to get hold of her letters. Ain't she spry, though, about pulling 'em open an' readin' 'em quick ! "

Mr. Ogden having passed some weeks in Edgecomb, could appreciate Miss Doane's eagerness to hear from her friends. It was however yet to be proven if it were she who had made upon him so lasting an impression.

" I should imagine your young lady would be lonely."

" She was kinder doleful at first, but my ! she's chipper as a cricket now. You'd oughter to see her a-startin' off over the bridge. She just goes it ! She don't act much like our Jane M'ria, always a-hangin' on to things," said the boy, scornfully, " an', by thunder, ain't she a beauty ? "

" Why, Jim, I had no idea you were such a critic of the fair sex," said Mr. Ogden, laughing.

" I rather guess I know when folks is good-lookin'. Jane M'ria says she's the image of the hotty Lady I-mer-gin. She's in one o' them *Ledger* yarns,

D

yer know. I never see I-mer-gin, an' I don't want ter, but this one's got yaller hair an' big black eyes. She an' I gits along first-rate," the little fellow continued confidentially. "I showed her the way to the ole fort; an' she takes lots o' things and goes over most ev'ry day."

"What do you mean by lots of things, Jimmie?"

"Well, she takes a readin'-book, an' a drawin'-book, an' a basket for leaves an' things, yer know, an' most ginrally a ombrell."

"Ah, she carries an umbrella, does she, this Miss L. L. Doane? A wise precautionary measure, certainly. She is no doubt a prudent young person. And what kind of an umbrella? Did you ever happen to notice it particularly?"

"It's got a shiny ball on top. Pewter, I guess. An' a pewter cross-piece on the handle. It's a real jolly little ombrell."

"Very jolly," said Mr. Ogden, with decision.

"Why, yer ain't seen it, have yer?" asked Jimmie, in surprise.

"No, I cannot say that I have ever actually seen it. But I have a remembrance of once holding in my hand an umbrella similar to the one you describe. And I coincide with your opinion that it is jolly—very jolly indeed. And, Jimmie, you are a fine boy You shall go down the river in my wherry as often as you like when I get out again. I think we are going to be excellent friends. Shake hands, Jimmie, and then you may run away."

Jimmie blushed with pleasure. He had never before been called a fine boy. He had never been in a wherry. He withdrew in a beatific state, and Mr. Ogden was left to his reflections.

"Circumstantial evidence is frequently at fault, but the chances are ten to one in favour of Jimmie's Miss Doane and my incognita being one and the same person."

He gained additional information when he received, the next day, this note. After reading it he gave a long, low, and expressive whistle.

MY DEAR PHILIP,—I have just learned with great rejoicing that you are rusticating in Edgecomb, the very place where I have left my fair sister, Miss Doane. I am detained here by business, and my wife and I cannot get down for a few weeks, which leaves Miss Doane in an unexpectedly lonely condition, and fills Mrs. Otis's heart with anxious forebodings. Under the circumstances, she ventures to send her compliments and say that she shall feel extremely grateful, and infinitely safer about Miss Doane, if you will have the kindness to call occasionally upon her, and if you would telegraph us in case of any accident or trouble of any kind, which we do not apprehend, of course ; but Miss Doane does not know a person in the place, and it is not agreeable for us to think of her as an exile, and we consequently hail you joyfully.

Harry Blake says he shall bring his yacht round there during the summer, and that he expects you to join him. We shall all be glad to see you again, and we'll have a magnificent reunion on the Idlewild.

As ever, yours, etc.,

TOM G. OTIS.

CHAPTER VI.

"Dost thou think I care for a satire or an epigram?"
Much Ado About Nothing.

THE Saturday of the week following the accident was a "gray day," with that soft, moist atmosphere which, inland, might predict rain, but which in Edgecomb was often but a mild intimation of the proximity of old Neptune. Grateful for the cloudiness which favoured his eyes and his plans, Mr. Ogden ventured out. He was in a cheerful frame of mind, and physically in a tolerably good condition, wearing only a "black and blue spot" of moderate size as a memento of Miss Doane's "jolly little ombrell."

Having inquired of Jimmie which was Miss Phipps's house, he started off at a brisk pace down the road which he lad last traversed under the peculiar circumstances recorded.

Jimmie's admiring face watched him from the porch.

Suddenly the young man's course was arrested by an—

"I say, wait for a feller, won't yer ?"

He waited, and Jimmie came springing towards him.

"Look here. If it's my girl you're after, she ain't likely to be ter home mornin's. The fort 's yer best dodge."

Looking pleasantly at this wise young judge, Mr. Ogden said—

" Jim, you are ' a youth whom fate reserves for a bright future.' Thank you for giving your information as you did, instead of from the steps, at the top of your voice."

" I ain't in the habit o' tellin' much to the women-folks, they make such a darned gabble."

His lofty air and precocious assumption of manly superiority were irresistible. Mr. Ogden laughed and asked him his age.

" Thirteen next July," was the prompt answer.

" Just twelve, then ? "

" Well, no, not precisely, I s'pose."

Here Mr. Ogden did Jimmie a momentary injustice. He concluded that the boy's genius as a profound observer of human nature was more remarkable than his knowledge of arithmetic. With a kindly, but wholly superfluous desire to straighten the little fellow's tangled ideas, he said—

" Why not? What day of the month was your birthday ? "

" 'Twasn't no day. It's goin' to be. It's a creepin' along thunderin' slow. It 's the thirty-first."

" Indeed ! You count more rapidly than most persons. As it is about the middle of July, I should say you were twelve years old, and an uncommonly smart boy at that."

" It depen's on how yer looks at it," Jimmie returned coolly. " Thirteen next July is about my kalkerlation."

" If you wish to grow old so fast, why do you not say you will be twenty-one, eight years from the thirty-first day of next July? It would be according to your principle, and might be still more encouraging than your view of the matter."

Jimmie knew that the gentleman was quizzing him, but adhered to his original line of argument.

"Cos 't ain't reasonable," he said stoutly, "and t' other way is. Yer see," he exclaimed, "I reckon from the Fourth. It's a jolly good day to start from. When the bells begin to ring next Fourth-of-July mornin', and the old cannon blazes away on the Common, I shall say to myself, 'Ole feller, you're fourteen next year, sure's yer born,' an' it keeps my spirits up wonderful."

"You deserve to be a second Methuselah, if you want to be. Good by, Jim. We understand each other, do we?"

"Mum's the word, sir," said the discreet boy; and Mr. Ogden resumed his walk.

Otis's letter, he thought, had lessened some of his difficulties. Presenting himself and his abject apologies before Miss Doane was less formidable now that her family sanctioned their acquaintance —even begged him to take a friendly interest in her. "I shall plead guilty, but recommend myself strongly to mercy. There is no getting round the awkwardness of the affair; but perhaps she'll be forgiving."

In this sanguine mood he approached Miss Phipps's abode. Miss Doane was out. Having left his card with the antique maiden, who at once put on her spectacles and severely scrutinized the name and the gentleman who bore it, he lighted a cigar and passed down the hill which led to the bridge. This ancient and honourable structure was nearly a mile in length and wide enough for three old-fashioned stage-coaches to drive abreast. It connected Edgecomb with an island, from which a second open bridge extended to the opposite village of Romney. The chain formed by the two bridges and the island was two miles and a half long; so that one, by going from Edgecomb to Romney and returning, could take a pleasant "constitutional" of five miles over the bridges, with their charming views both up and down the river, and through the fragrant wood-road that ran across the island.

In Edgecomb's golden days its bridge was a famous promenade and place of resort. There at sunset the people would gather—old and young, rich and poor—to walk, to talk, to see and be seen, to watch the long light sweep across the wide river and fade away behind the hills.

"There youths and maidens dreaming strayed."

There rose castles in the air without number. There hearts were broken, sweet and bitter words were said, and many sad farewells. It was a gloomy old bridge crowded with phantoms; but not one ghost of the past disturbed Philip Ogden's peace of mind. He was glad to be a free man again. The outer world looked pleasant to him after his dull week in the farm-house. The dead past was nothing to him, and his thoughts of the bridge were altogether practical and commonplace. He noticed that its timbers were rotten, its railing feeble and tottering—dying of old age, and the

"selectmen" would not give it any Elixir of Life
in the shape of energetic repairs. He saw one
patch of fresher wood, where a heavily laden
stage-coach went through some years previous.
"Comfortable predicament for the passengers. I
believe somebody told me the accident had not a
tragical termination. No lives were lost, nor bones
broken, but I am not surprised that stages cross
Edgecomb bridge no more." It probably was not
really worth repairing. To let it alone or rebuild
it completely was the only thing to be done, and
Edgecomb had apparently decided upon the former
course. How long before it would fall? He leaned over the railing and looked at the mouldering
trestle-work, then glanced idly at the countless
initials, carved years and years before—some perhaps by laughing children trooping noisily down
from school, some by happy lovers who stood there
dreamily watching the moon rise over the hills, and
asking blindly of the future what it would never
give them. The quaint letters and symbols spoke
a language which Philip, in his tranquil mood, failed to interpret. He regarded unfeelingly a heart
pierced by numerous arrows—a pitiful design, em-
blematic, no doubt, of much suffering. An old
farmer in a creaking waggon, jogging over to Edgecomb, nodded familiarly, after the country fashion,
to the young man, who responded pleasantly and
went on his way.

He reached the island, and turned off from the
main road which crossed it into a winding path
which ran through the woods. Soon he came to
an opening. Here the land began to rise percepti-

bly towards the southern point of the island, where
a curious excavation, an old embankment, and frag-
ments of a wall marked the site of the fort.

He had not before visited this spot, and was surprised at the extent of the view. West was Edgecomb, thick with elms on its hill-slope, crowned by
a row of stately, sombre houses and three white
church spires. On the east, Romney ; and beyond
each village the pretty hills rising higher and higher in the distance ; while from his elevated position
he could follow the graceful shore-line many miles.

"This is fine, but I presume I lose half of it. I
must bring a glass over here to-morrow." He
turned, walked a few steps leisurely in the direction of Romney, when he saw directly before him
an object which he needed no glass to appreciate.
Leaning against a rock, looking as guileless as if it
had never been an instrument of torture, was an
umbrella—*the* umbrella he could not well doubt.
He took it up and examined it with pardonable
curiosity. It was a small black silk one, with an
ebony stick, having on one end a silver cross, on the
other the silver ball that did "millions of mischief";
and the missing link in the chain of evidence stared
him in the face from a silver band on which was
engraved, "L. L. Doane."

He was extremely amused. He struck the palm
of his left hand lightly with that ornamental ball,
estimated its weight, and felt that he was a lucky
man. "If I were in reality Miss Doane's guardian," he thought, smilingly, "I would take effec-
tual measures to keep her in the house stormy evenings, not only for her own sake, but out of regard for
the safety of the public."

He inferred that she must be in the vicinity. She probably had gone into the wood for flowers. He might miss her should he seek her there. He would await her return. Thus he reasoned, and serenely anticipated making a pleasant acquaintance.

Birch Point, one of the loveliest spots on the shore below Edgecomb, was seen from the fort to the best advantage.

"Perhaps Miss Doane will allow me to take her out rowing. She might like that quiet little cove over there. Ladies do not generally fancy too much current." Certainly she might rely upon him for any amusement he could afford her. She had the strongest claim upon his services. There was nothing that he would not do for Otis, and nothing half good enough to do for her, in atonement for his insolence. He presumed she would be an agreeable girl. Otis's wife's sister ought to be. That was, to be sure, a woman's method of reasoning, but he fancied it would prove correct in this instance. A strong ludicrous element at the beginning of an acquaintance was often of use. It gave one a foundation to build upon.

In this state of benign composure, making plans as to drives and rows which he hoped would meet with Miss Doane's gracious approval, he seated himself on the rock and took a cigar from his case. As he turned to strike a match, an open sketch-book suddenly arrested his attention. The grayish tint of its leaves blended with the rock on which it was lying, and had it not been near him it would have escaped his notice. He gazed as if spellbound. He was a man of honour, scrupulous in trifles, yet he took that book in his two hands and intently scrutinized each line on the pages before him. "Every man has his price," is an unpleasant misanthropical doctrine. It is more agreeable, and perhaps as wise in the end, to forget it, and dwell kindly upon the vast amount of temptation poor human nature is sometimes enabled to resist. Here was, no doubt, a real temptation to Philip Ogden, and it would have been highly creditable to him had he, with his usual delicacy, virtuously closed the book. But that vigorous, dashing style of drawing was his price. He did not resist. He succombed completely. He was even guilty of the enormous misdemeanour of reading what was written as a motto for the sketches. And then this misguided man threw back his head and laughed loud and long, laughed as he had not since he was a boy and had successfully carried out some madcap prank at school.

"She's a veritable genius!" he said. "She would make a fortune for any illustrated newspaper in the world. It is the richest thing I ever saw."

At the top of a page were, wickedly misapplied, Shelley's lines, —-

> "We look before and after,
> And pine for what is not."

"BEFORE"

was the title of the first sketch, which depicted this scene :—

A pouring rain. A sharp corner where two vil-

lage streets meet, the one with an ascending, the
other with a descending slope.   Upon what might
be called the down-grade, advancing furiously, was
a female figure drawn with much spirit.   Her draperies were flying in the wind.   Her umbrella,
grasped in both hands, had a malignant, evil look,
—an umbrella rampant,—her resolute poise told
of contest with the storm, and strong determination
to go on in spite of it.   While upon the other street,
unconscious of his doom, sauntering complacently
to meet it, was a man, and such a man!   It was
here that the genius of the artist had most forcibly ·
asserted itself.   A dandy.   A Turveydrop.   A man
with his hat set jauntily on the side of his head.
A man whose buttonhole bouquet resembled a display of " mammoth " vegetables, who looked as if
he pointed his toes when he walked and had
devoted an hour to his necktie, and whose face was
devoid of all meaning except the unutterable self-
sufficiency shown in the lines about the mouth.   In
this picture collision was imminent, and upon the
next page its results were portrayed in

"AFTER."

A rough, hilly country-road, with gloomy woods
on both sides.   Through wind and rain walk, arm
in arm, the two figures described.   The surprised,
indignant remonstrance in the girl's face was a
study.   The man, the upper part of his face being
concealed by a handkerchief bound round his eyes,
still disclosed the turned-up corners of his odious
mouth, and minced along pompously, while—most

malicious touch of all!—he held an umbrella well over his own head, and in exactly the position that would entail constant drippings on his companion's. In the corner of each sketch was plainly written, L. L. Doane. Thus had she revenged herself.

CHAPTER VII.

"What, my dear Lady Disdain! Are you yet living?"
Much Ado About Nothing.

PHILIP, engrossed by this masterly work of art, did not hear a step on the soft turf.

"When you have quite finished your inspection, sir, I will trouble you for my sketchbook," said a voice behind him dryly, and with a sarcastic inflection that was unmistakable.

In an instant he threw away his cigar, sprang to his feet, turned, took off his hat, and saw what he never in after years forgot. A slight graceful figure in soft brown, standing erect before him, with a wide flat basket filled with wild-flowers, ferns and mosses. Beneath a brown shade-hat, pushed back from the face, wavy fair hair, a pale olive skin, great dark eyes looking coldly at him, and a mouth at that moment set haughtily in a manner that boded no good.

Politely and inquiringly he said,—

"Miss Doane?"

She was a truthful girl, but her good angel forsook her, and she told a white lie.

"You have the advantage of me, sir."

She could not swear, possibly, that his name was Ogden, but she had every reason to think that it was. Did not that discoloured cheek prove his iden-

tity ? He was not appalled by her icy demeanor,
which involuntarily reminded him of the " hotty
Lady I-mer-gin," and, restraining a smile which he
felt would not be well received by this severely
statuesque young lady, he replied,—

"Pardon me.   The advantage was certainly
yours before.   It is yours now.   It must of necessity always remain with you."

Miss Doane in her varied reading had never met
with the Lady Imogen, whom she was supposed to
resemble, and she misinterpreted the cause of the
faint smile upon Mr. Ogden's lips.   Neither his
cordial voice, nor his genial allusion to their first
meeting, nor the eminently conciliatory character
of his remark, found favour with her.   Without
replying, without indeed glancing at him, she
stooped, took from the rock a small volume which
had been concealed by the sketch-book, and which,
carefully lifting her violets and ferns, she placed in
her basket.   She then passed by him for her umbrella.   Her movements were deliberate, and it
was evident, preparatory to departure.

Philip realised that she was going because he
had come.   His intentions in visiting her favourite
haunt were, as has been shown, most amicable.
The weapon that had wounded him he had sur-
veyed in a forgiving, even in a quizzical spirit.
The caricature, so clear an exponent of Miss Doane's
impression of him, he had examined with impur-
turable good-nature, admiring the humorous talent
it displayed, and sympathising with the incensed
artist.   " I do not wonder that she thought me a
prig," was his amiable comment when studying the

unflattering sketches. But her continued silence, under the circumstances agressive in itself, her indescribable frigidity, and her affectatation of ignoring his presence, were enough to irritate the meekest man. The genial look faded from his face. And she quite exhausted his patience when she finally said in an exasperatingly indifferent way, standing before him and looking, not at him, but with still eyelids and a fixed gaze far beyond him down upon the river,—

"Will you have the kindness to give me my book ? "

He had unconsciouely retained it.

With more serious apologies, he felt that to ask her pardon for examining her sketches might not be superfluous. He thought also of Tom's letter, and of his own object in seeking her, an honest desire to atone as far as possible for the past by the proffer of unlimited service in future. But her hauteur forbade the expression of his sentiments. It seemed that an allusion to things of the past was precisely what she wished to avoid.

"So be it then. A man cannot talk to a statue cut in alabaster. Any reference to Tom is out of the question. She scorns to conceal that I am repugnant to her. Having no merits of my own, I have no desire to prop myself up with Otis's. The briefer the interview the better for both parties ! "

Such were his hasty reflections as she demanded her property. For one moment he looked steadily at her, then placed the book in her hand, and in a tone quite as cold as her own, said simply,—

" It is my place, Miss Doane, not yours, to withdraw." Lifting his hat with grave courtesy, he walked rapidly away and soon disappeared among the trees.

So they met again, and so they parted.

Had she received him with that gentle effusion and highly flattering manner which most men esteem "an excellent thing in woman," had she tenderly sympathized with his misfortune, deprecatingly explained why she was out in the storm that night, disarmed him with an appealing look from under her long lashes, and a "Was it so very naughty?" in an infantine, confiding tone, she might have impressed him with the idea that she was the sweetest, most artless girl in existence; that wandering about alone dark, stormy nights was, in her, a praiseworthy act, and destroying people's visual organs a fascinating accomplishment. Results equally astounding have been attained by young women less clever than Leigh Doane, with men quite as sensible as Philip Ogden. But she was twenty, and well grown, and she did not know how to assume ways which are, as was Richard III., "too childish-foolish for this world." Her cleverness did not lie in the knowledge of such tactics. She had not studied them, nor did she, as do some women, know them intuitively. There was, however, another, a medium course, and one that would have been in accordance with her nature. She could have been frank and sufficiently gracious. She might have accepted his apologies and made her own. Though disliking him, she could at least have been civil. For reasons best known to herself, she was not. And these two, who might have

E

engaged in a bland conversation upon topics of mutual interest,—the weather, the scenery, why Tom did not come, why Mr. Ogden had, how queer Miss Phipps was, and what rare specimens of humanity were revealed in the Holbrook family,—lost their opportunity. One was left alone. The other, having abandoned the regular path, was going through the woods with great strides, accelerated by indignation, trampling over the underbrush, and pushing away low branches with marked energy. His course, as he had anticipated, brought him out at a point in the main road not far from the Romney bridge, and presently its loose planks were rattling beneath his tread. He crossed it, and in a long ramble on the east side of the river walked off his vexation, and coolly decided that Miss Doane and her vagaries were of small consequence.

He had been prepared to blame himself wholly, her not at all ; but her ungracious reception had led him to think that the scales might be more evenly balanced, that his week of inconvenience and pain, his hearty desire to make reparation for his blundering, might justly have some weight in his favour. As a gentleman, he must always regret having caused her so much discomfort and annoyance ; but since she had not even allowed him the satisfaction of calling himself a brute, since she had rendered expiation impossible, he washed his hands of the whole matter. He had done his part. Angels could do no more.

Edgecomb air was as healthful, Edgecomb waters afforded as fine facilities for rowing, as before the advent of this Miss Doane, who was, by the way, a charmingly agreeable person to take out in his wherry. Should the boat upset, she would float about in the water like any other iceberg. His feeling towards her gradually merged [into quiet disapproval. What he knew of her he did not admire, except, of course, her beauty. That, he admitted, was of a rare order. It was not the style he liked best. It had not the sweet, winning, ever-varying expression that he preferred. But in an artistic sense simply, Miss Doane's face was the most beautiful he had ever seen. And whether it was on account of its intrinsic beauty, or because he had not before noticed a lovely girl in Edgecomb, or because she was the first woman who had rendered it quite evident to him that in her opinion he was intolerably disagreeable, it haunted him. In spite of what he assured himself was pure indifference to her, like a familiar picture he could see, well defined before him, the background of trees, the dull skies, the soft brown of her dress, the great basket laden with cool green things from the woods, the long vines trailing over its edge, and, most distinct of all, the fair young face, so fresh in its colouring, so inflexible in its frozen repose.

What can she want of violets? It was winsome Persephone who gathered flowers on the meadow— not an ice-maiden like this. Even Rappacini's daughter, nourished upon poison, and withering flowers with her fatal breath, was less chilling and unlovely in manner.

Meanwhile the forbidding, repellent, self-poised

creature sat in a dejected heap on the grass—elbows on the rock, face on her hands, sad eyes looking off absently across the water at Birch Point. Already the iceberg, humanized, was suffering the cruel pangs of remorse. She had been inexcusably rude to Mr. Ogden, and she liked neither him nor herself any the better for that.

"O dear, I wish they would come!" she sighed.

CHAPTER VIII.

"So we met
In this old sleepy town, at unaware,
The man and I."
—BROWNING.

EDGECOMB, July 15, 18—.

DEAR TOM AND DEAREST BESSIE,—Let us play "Consequences." I'll begin.

Miss Laura Leigh Doane and Mr. Philip Ogden met in Edgecomb, on a street-corner, a dark, stormy night, to the physical distress of one and the mental agony of the other.

HE SAID,—

"My good woman, your insignificant umbrella has had the presumption to put out my majestic eye. Shall I graciously allow you the supreme honour of trudging through two miles of mud with me?"

SHE SAID,—

(meekly, but with rage, hate, rebellion, and various other deadly sins warring in her heart,)—

"Yes, sir."

THE WORLD SAID,—

(or would have said, had it known anything about it, what it has ever said since Adam introduced the custom of accusing "the woman;")—

"She had only herself to blame."

, The Consequences Were :—

Mr. Ogden retired from the world for a season,
and Miss Doane indulged in hatred, malice, and
all uncharitableness. She never, never wished to
meet him again. And when at last he loomed up
suddenly before her, she was unpardonably rude
and disagreeable ; yet not so utterly lost to every
semblance of good feeling that she could thus ill-
treat a friend of Tom without repenting in sack-
cloth and ashes, and longing for her dear people to
come and brush away her cobwebs.

Bessie, dear, this is true, or nearly so, and it is
what you have thought only my nonsense when I
have just touched upon it or fluttered over it in my
letters. I ought to have told you before, but it did
seem too ridiculous to write. Indeed, I will re-
serve the details of my escapade until I can talk
with you ; but I did go out in the rain. I did run
against him. I did hurt him. And he thought I
was a nobody, and coolly requested me to tie a
bandage over his eyes and take him home, which I
did, to my own profound amazement. He thanked
me, and *feed me well.* (And when you come,
Tom, you must give the odious creature his ill
timed offering.) This was the evening of the day
you did not come. You cannot understand it, nor
can I ; but it all happened. I went for a book,
you see, and everything worked against me,—even
the powers of the air,—and it was all so very un-
comfortable for me afterwards. I could not help
attributing it to Mr. Ogden ; and that was why I
told you, Tom, not to send him to see me.

I have reversed the usual order of things. First
I made war, then I declared it. I have been detestable ; but, Tom, what you can find to admire in
that man is beyond my feeble comprehension.

He was confined to his room a week or more, so
my little Jimmie-boy reported. During that time
I became quite softened. I could not like his
Grand Mogul ways, but I was so sorry, so very,
very sorry that I had actually hurt him, and that
he was suffering some pain, no doubt, and much
loneliness, and all through my evil-doings. Then
came your last letters insisting earnestly upon my
knowing him, telling me that he was such an " uncommonly good fellow " (Tom, if he's " uncommonly good," commonly good is more to my taste),
and assuring me that you would feel much relieved
about me if so fine, high-toned, honourable, efficient, altogether charming and admirable individual
would deign to keep himself informed of my movements, and would telegraph to you in case I should
fall from a rock and break my neck, or lean too
hard upon the railing of the dear dilapidated old
bridge. Perhaps I did not fully appreciate the
practical utility of this plan; but since you really
wished me to know him, and especially since you
announced that you had written to him desiring
him, formally, to call upon me, I grew decently
amiable. I reasoned with myself. I decided to
meet him frankly, to express my regret for the accident, to treat the matter of my performing escort-
duty for him as of no consequence at all, in short,
to be very good during his visit, which I naturally
thought would take place here, at the house ; and

afterwards I would see him as little as possible, I determined.

I was prepared to do all that could be expected of me ; to sit like a model from a Book of Decorum, with my reluctant vertebræ leaning against one of Phipps's perpendicular chair-backs ; to converse as well as I knew how upon any topic which might prove agreeable to my guest. But I was not—I was not prepared for the sight that met my eyes yesterday at the fort.

I had been in the woods for flowers, and returning to my favourite resting-place saw a gentleman—Mr. Odgen, I knew instinctively—intently regarding my sketch-book. His back was turned, so that I could not see his face, but I knew he was laughing, for his shoulders fairly shook. Indeed, I have the impression that he must have shouted over my designs, for I heard something of the kind when I was in among the trees. I will do him the justice to say that the book was lying open when he found it. And, Bessie, fancy at what !—(the influences, as the mediums say, must have been sadly against me that morning)—at some absurd sketches illustrative of our first meeting. I did them the day after the accident, and he was as ridiculous as I could make him. It was for your amusement, not his. He had no right to laugh ! Yesterday my work was only an innocent, amiable little sketch of Birch Point, a fascinating subject I am constantly attempting. Why did he not see that instead ? Why did the leaves open to the malicious, naughty caricatures I had almost forgotten ? Why did I not close the book ? I

usually do. Because the man is my evil genius.
Before he appears I do some unfortunate, unnatural thing. When I am with him I am completely
transformed. I do not recognise myself. Scold
me, Tom, as much as you like. I deserve it, but if
you love me, come down and keep him away.

Where was I ? O—just coming down from the
woods. Bessie, I am sorry, too sorry for what I
did. I do not seek to excuse the inexcusable. If
patient Griselda's liege lord—tyrannical old Turk
that he was !—had chosen to swing her about by
the hair of her head as light exercise and pastime,
I presume, from all accounts, the poor thing, for
whom I never had the faintest spark of admiration, would have meekly borne it, and sweetly
encouraged him in it, so long as there was a hair left
for him to grasp; but I am not sure that even she
would have seen a perfect stranger examining at
his leisure her own private property, without making a mild protest, and to me the sight was intolerably provoking.

There he sat on my rock, surrounded, like a
Choctaw chieftain, with trophies of victory. My
Idyls at his right. My umbrella leaning against
the rock at his left. My sketch-book open in his
hands. It was too much. The tide of memory
rushed over me. I was again seized with the intense unreasoning dislike I had felt for him. Was
I always to appear at a disadvantage before him ?
I am ashamed to tell you how disagreeably I advanced and demanded my book. I wickedly
hoped he would be confused. He never dreamed
of such a thing. He is always so unpleasantly

" superior." He rose to meet me with a cordial expression, as if I were an old and valued friend. I determined to ruffle that beautiful composure. I did not know I could be so detestable ; but a latent talent of that description, I suppose, like courage, " mounteth with occasion." By my man ner, I said as plainly as by words, " Do not apologize. Do not introduce yourself. Do not speak. You are odious. I am going."

I pretended not to look at him, but I saw per fectly well his expression changing from smiling ease to gravity, severity, as it dawned upon him that my inimical bearing was with malice prepense. He gave me one long, steady look, as if to discover to what species of created beings I belonged, then with a word left me. Your Mr. Ogden has quick perceptions, Tom. Any man of sense would have understood me ; but I think some men would have insisted upon speaking.

And, after all, he had the best of it. He was still " superior." He went through the woods, it is true, with great rapidity, suggestive, it may be, of inward wrath, but he made his exit from this dramatic scene with calmness, grace, and dignity. He did not forget that an impressive deportment is always the best policy. His final remark was a rebuke in its cool civility, for you see I was cool in civility personified. He meant to conduct himself as irreproachably as a Bayard, whatever caprice my waywardness might develop, and I was capricious and unreasonable as a child with a grown-up capa city for being disagreeable. He was right, I was wrong. My head tells me this, while my heart

rises up in wrath against him. How sorry you
will both be ! Would you believe it ? I tried not
to care when I saw that great purplish mark in
his cheek. I could not help feeling distressed,
though I endeavoured to look as stony as a sphinx.

If it were not for him, Edgecomb would be
Paradise. But I suppose an earthly one must always have a serpent, and every little Miss Muffit,
a great black spider to come in the way. He is
the spider that drives me from my curds and whey.
Won't somebody have the kindness to step on
him ?

These long, quiet days here are too beautiful. I
find some lovely spot and read a little, draw a little, dream a little, and think that you will be here
soon to intensify my happiness ; and the trees and
hills and waters are so noble, "the birds and the
flowers are so kind," that it all seems like an enchanted life, until suddenly I remember my misdeeds, and the beautiful illusion is destroyed. I
cannot be happy here any more. Jimmie is my
only human comfort. He is, I tell him, a rough
diamond, and hereafter I shall spell his name with
a G. He is not, perhaps, "of the purest ray
serene," still he is precious and sparkling, though
unpolished, and he shall be Gem, not Jim. Dear
child ! He seems to have the most incomprehensible fancy for me. He left a handful of colum-
bines with Miss Phipps for me, long before I was
awake one morning ; and he went ever so many
miles for a pretty species of fern which he had
heard me say I was sorry I could not find in this
vicinity. He is very bright, merry, and amusing,

and has a loving heart and an appreciative nature; though he seemed to me in the first place nothing more than a comical, impudent little ragamuffin. Now I perceive respect for me and affection shining out through the outward roughness,—the marvellous language and want of training.

When *do* you think you will come? If you do not intend to start in a day or two, mayn't I, please may I not, go home? I could act as escort for you, Bessie, and bring you down quite as well as Tom can, if he would only think so; and it would be so much better than staying here, and dreading to stir for fear of meeting Mr. Ogden, and doing or saying some fatal thing which it never entered my head to do or say before.

> " Up the airy mountain,
> Down the rushy glen,
> We dare na go a-huntin',
> For fear of—" P. Ogden.

I wish he would go away! I am penitent, very penitent, but I never wish to see him again. Literally,

> " Every prospect pleases, and only man is vile."

Come to me, or let me go to you, is the prayer of

Your loving

LEIGH.

CHAPTER IX.

" Still harping."
—Hamlet.

"MISS LEIGH, we got this in a field to Birch Point. Yer don't want it, do yer? Yer wouldn't like it, would yer? Yer couldn't stick it in yer hat, could yer? Say!"

Miss Doane took the long black feather from the boy's hand, and smiled at his eagerness.

"It is very pretty, Gem. What is it?"

"A eagle's."

"An eagle's, really? 'As a feather is wafted downward from an eagle in his flight,'" she repeated dreamily, standing in the open doorway and glancing far up above the elm-tops, as if she could see the slender thing descending through the air. Then, to the boy: "Certainly, I would like it, Gem, and thank you very much. I never saw one before. How very glossy it is, and even, as if its edge were cut with a knife!"

"I s'pose yer don't want to put it in yer hat, do yer?" said Gem, with pleased, smiling eyes, while his mouth twitched violently in his effort to look indifferent.

"Who was it who wore an eagle's plume? Rob Roy? Far better it would suit a brave Highland chieftain than a commonplace young woman like me. But since the noble bird will not suspect to what base use we have put it, I'll see what can be done to please you, my dear."

She ran up stairs and returned in a moment with a small black hat and her work-basket, and, seated in the doorway, with Jimmie on a lower step, she tried the effect of his last offering at her shrine.

"Gem, it's too long.   I shall look as tall as Mrs. Giantess Blunderbore."

" Let's cut it."

" It would be a pity to do that, unless I could use both parts.   I do not like to throw away what a friend brings me.   It is neither pleasant nor polite, is it, Gem ?   Ah, I know !   The tip I will put in my hat, quietly, you see, with an unob-trusive, deprecating expression, so any mighty eagle soaring about will not spy it and feel in-sulted, and pounce down and peck my eyes out ; and the other I will make into a most beautiful quill pen.   However it may write, the association of ideas will be very high-toned indeed.   A great, glorious eagle,—how much more inspiring his quill ought to be than that of a common goose ! There, Gem, how is that ? "   And she put on the hat, with the little black tip standing up jauntily behind some bows.   " Is it about right ?   Then I'll fasten it."   And off came the hat.

" I told him yer'd like it.   I said yer'd put it in yer hat, and now yer have, haven't yer ? " said Jimmie, ecstatically.

Miss Doane bent her face over her work.

" Told whom, Gem ? "

"Mr. Ogden. He picked it up an' was a goin' to drop it over the bank, an' I said I wanted it for you."

Miss Doane coloured furiously. It would be too childish not to wear it now; but how she did want to pull it out! 'After all she reflected, it had really nothing to do with Mr. Ogden. She would wear it, and only remember little Gem's kindness.

"He's tip-top, Miss Leigh. You an' him are the best fellers I ever see."

"Gem," said the girl, gravely, "I'm not a feller, and you should say saw instead of see."

Unabashed, Gem continued,—

"Mr. Ogden, he got off a mighty queer yarn yesterday when I told him I knowed yer'd like the feather cos yer allers liked the things I had brung. He thought as how yer wouldn't want it, yer know, and says he—"

"Knew, not knowed, and brought, not brung," said Miss Doane, oracularly.

The importance of improving Jim's English was at certain moments singularly urgent, The tide of her criticism, however, seemed to ebb and flow in a spasmodic, eccentric manner.

Sometimes he would chatter by the hour with never a word of correction from her.

"Yes'm," said Gem, dutifully. "Says he, 'Did yer ever read about—' 'bout a—wait an I'll tell yer—it was real funny—says he—"

"Gem, how would you like to ramble off somewhere with me? This is too fine a morning to waste in the house, or even out here on the steps. We'll have a lovely outing, you and I; and if Miss

Phipps will give us some lunch, we'll go off for the day. Would you like it?"

" Wouldn't I though?"

" Very well; wait till I get my shawl and pack a basket. A small and select picnic like this will be charming. You shall go where you like. My fate is in your hands. I want to see an entirely new spot."

" All right," said Gem, cheerily. "I guess I know what will hit your case. Him an' me was down there, an' he thought as how it was a pooty likely sort of a place. Says he—"

" Excuse me, Gem, but I must go and beg Miss Phipps for some things for our basket." And Leigh sprang up quickly and vanished through an inner door.

Gem sat down on the steps, scowled, and thought vigorously. Presently he shouted, "I say! Miss Leigh!" She appeared at the dining-room door. As well hope to stem a torrent with a straw as to interpose such trifles as grammatical errors and lunch-baskets in the way of Gem's inevitable recital.

" Well, dear," she said patiently. Perhaps after the child had freed his mind he would be willing to turn his attention in some other direction.

" Kim-eleon was the word. Kimeleon. Says he, 'Did yer ever read about a kimeleon?' Says I, 'No.' Says he, 'It's a curious animal, an' you may look in my dictionary for it when we go home, an' then you'll] know another fack in nateral history, my boy.' Says I, 'Is it like a eagle?' Says he, 'Not in the least. It is a animal that changes its colour more or less with the colour of objects about it, an' with its temper when disturbed.' He said it to me twice, an' I saw it in his big dictionary afterwards, an' I learned the spellin' an' the meanin'. There was a plaguy long word—"

"Gem," said Leigh, reprovingly.

" Well, awful long then. It was pre-hen-sile. Its tail is prehensile. That means it can hang on to things like blazes. Mr. Ogden said that fack didn't interest him pertickerly. What he liked to meditate upon was, that its colour varied as its temper was disturbed. I was a-studyin' of it out loud up in his room, yer know, an' he was a smokin', an' he larfed an' larfed. He said some folks was like the kimeleon."

Miss Doane bit her lip, looked very straight, and waited for the boy to communicate his newly acquired knowledge.

"Yes, dear ; that is very interesting. Perhaps I may be able some time to give you equally valuable information. At present our basket is the more important topic. If you and I are hungry, we won't feel like improving our minds, will we, Gem ? You may come in, if you like, and help me. Here I am like Charlotte, cutting bread and butter."

"Charlotte who ? "

"Charlotte—, I'm sure I don't know what her other name was, and it does not matter, my dear ; for her story would make you neither so merry as that of Mrs. Giantess Blunderbore, nor so wise as the dictionary definition of a chameleon, so I shall not tell it to you, Jimmie-boy."

F

"Do yer want that hunk o' meat, an' them cook-ies an' things in ? "

" Child ! Child ! Not without a napkin. Things one eats should look pretty. There,—this is the way. First the napkin, then the meat, sliced thin, so, between two plates. Why, Gem, could you really eat it, dumped in your way ? "

" Course, I could. What's the use o' yer nap-kins ? Yer can't eat 'em."

" Gem, you are an untutored little savage. Why, do you know I am sometimes very much ashamed to eat at all, right in the face and eyes of a beau-tiful landscape ? It seems so presuming, such a desecration. But there's something in the air here that gives one an unconscionable appetite.—Miss Phipps, you are exceedingly kind. The cream will be very acceptable.—Gem, run out and get me a little bunch of sweet-peas. We cannot eat them, but the bit of bright shall serve to beautify our feast, and to elevate your ideas, you benighted boy. —I may have them, may I not, Miss Phipps ? Nothing more, thank you."

They started off merrily. Miss Phipps gave a shrill parting charge from the door :—

" You be keerful about bringin' back them things, will yer ? "

" O, certainly ! " replied Leigh, smilingly. " We will take excellent care of everything. And," turn-ing to Jim, " you are going to take care of me, are you not ? Do you know, Gem, you should offer to take my shawl and the books and the umbrella, as well as the basket. I should not think of allowing you to carry them all, of course, but the offer ought in propriety to be made. The shawl, you see, hangs easily over my shoulder, the umbrella I wish to use ; you and I together can swing the basket as Jack and Jill did the pail when they went up the hill ; and the strap, if you please, you may take in your other hand. Still, Gem, you must offer to carry everything."

"What for ?" said the matter-of-fact Jimmie. " Just as lief lug 'em all as not, but I ain't got but two hands, an' ef yer've fixed things 'bout as yer want 'em, what's the use of talkin' ?"

"Gem, Gem, you have yet to learn the use of the beautiful. Courtesy, my child, demands that you offer and that I decline. Exactly why, I am not sure that I know myself. It is a little polite social fiction, you see. However, I will excuse you till next time."

The boy listened with a bright admiring look. Her words were new and strange to him. · Her meaning he rarely failed to grasp.

"Miss Leigh, you an' him talk jest precisely alike."

"Gem," said she, abruptly, " I think I never saw more beautiful clouds. They look like great snowy mountains, do they not ? Alpine summits."

" I know all about 'em," was the complacent response to this burst of enthusiasm. "He told me. Them's the cumulus. Heaps an' heaps on 'em ain't they, and jolly white ?"

Leigh sighed despairingly. Could she never be free from this incubus ? Did it extend even to the clouds ?

" Why, Gem, it is towards Birch Point we are going, is it not ?"

" It is to Birch Point, if yer don't mind the walk. We're goin' the short cut. 'Tain't more'n three or four miles this way. Him an' me went t' other way, an' he—"

" You dear little Gem, I would be delighted to go! I have tried to sketch Birch Point from the fort. Now I can see how the fort looks from the Point."

" There's a cave there. Him an' me went down in. He is awful knowin'. He's learned me a pile of things. Says he—"

" Taught me," instantly corrected the oracle.

" I rather guess you an' him together will make a stunnin' scholar of me," said Jim, with a chuckle.

" 'You an' him together!' Worse and worse," thought she. Severe criticism had failed to divert Jimmie's ideas. Would a downright compliment be of any use, she wondered.

" It is a pleasure to teach you anything, you are so bright and remember so well," she graciously remarked.

" Well, he says I'm bright. I'm a awful block-head at school, though. Funny, ain't it?"

"I think you are very bright," said Leigh, reso-lutely, ignoring the ever-present " he." " You ought to make a very clever man. There may be a few things I can teach you now, but if you work in the right way, you will know ever so much more than I do when you are twenty."

"Twenty? Are you twenty? He's thirty." Leigh groaned in spirit. " I asked him, an' he told me, but he larfed and said I mustn't ask folks how old they was, pertickerly ladies, so I didn't ask you— but I wanted to know awfully, cos yer kinder young and kinder old, yer know. Sometimes yer don't seem no older'n me, an' sometimes yer act as old as the parson. I asked him how old he s'posed you was, an' he said he s'posed nothing whatever. ' Far be it from me,' says he, ' to presume to have any opinion on that subjeck.' An' he kinder larfed. Odd talkin' chap, ain't he ? "

Leigh, in utter hopelessness, remained silent. It was evidently useless to attempt to turn the conversation into any channel which would not immediately lead to her bugbear and Gem's hero.

On they walked, swinging the basket between them. Suddenly, Gem said,—

" *He* said ' clever.' I told yer, him an' you talked alike. He said, with the right trainin' I'd make a clever feller."

" O Gem, Gem, if you only would not, quite all the time ! " thought Leigh.

" An' I thought clever meant kinder good-natured, but he told me it was jest the same as knowin'."

A smile was her only response.

" Yer see, I'm considerable 'stonished, cos I kinder got settled into thinkin' I was a noodle," confided Jimmie, with his head on one side, and casting a curious little canary-bird look up into her face. " Jones, he stuck to it three winters," continued Gem, laughing, " an' I begun to think p'r'aps he was right about it, if he was most gen'rally a darn fool."

"Jimmie, really this is dreadful. You promised not to use such words," said Miss Doane, with dignity.

" Well, I won't, then," said Jim, half in peni-
tence, half in mischief. " I'm awful sorry." Then,
the mischief predominating, " I won't say 'em
about any other feller if yer'll let me 'bout Jones,
an' I don't care pertickerly for darn if yer like
pesky any better, or thunderin', or any sech."

Jim's naïveté, as usual, proved irresistible. The
dignity vanished, and Leigh, laughing, inquired—

" Who is this poor Mr. Jones who is doomed to
be called such naughty names ? "

" He's the schoolmaster," replied Gem, with
sublime contempt. " He don't know so much as
once. The biggest noony yer ever did see," said
he, with tremendous energy. " He cum down from
Ayerville College with his hair parted in the middle.
He talkth thith way, an' thays ' my de-ah ' to the
girls. Kisses 'em too, by thunder, when he thinks
folks ain't round, an' lots of the big fellers licked
him last winter, an' I rather guess he ain't a-comin'
this way again. Not much, old doughface ! " he
added with a sneer.

Leigh's spirits rose. Here, at last, was an all-
engrossing topic upon which Gem should dilate at
his pleasure. Contempt for the schoolmaster should
be encouraged.

" So Mr. Jones thought that you were not
bright. He was mistaken, Gem, utterly mistaken."

" Well, yer see I was kinder young an' small
when he begun," said Gem, drawing himself up and
looking as tall as possible. " It was considerable
time ago,—three years last winter. Bein' only a
little shaver, I was mortal 'fraid if he learned me

anything he knowed, I'd grow up into jest such
another noodle. So I kinder got into the habit of
losin' my books, an' never knowin' nothin' at all,
an' runnin' away every chance I got, an' I kep' it
up pretty stiddy all the time the old donkey
stayed."

Leigh was aware that she ought to remonstrate,
but she felt a surprising sympathy with Jim, shar-
ing his dislike for the absent Jones, and she laughingly said,—

" What a comfort you must have been to the
poor man ! "

" Ruther guess I was. Heaps o' comfort. He
forgot to tell me so, though," said Gem, with a
queer expression, as if recalling days gone by and
scenes with the " marster." " I can't help it," he
exclaimed vehemently ; " when I don't like folks I
won't learn a blessed thing, an' that's the end on
it ; but," he added with immense enthusiasm, " if
you an' Mr. Ogden, you an' him, both of you together—"

Leigh had been breathing freely for a few moments. Here she actually shuddered.

" If two reggler bricks like you an' he want me
to peg away at books an' things, I'll do it sure's
yer born."

Miss Doane threw her shawl upon the grass and
sat down.

" Tired ? "

" Not physically tired, Gem, but mentally stun-
ned. As the French say, ' I can no more.' " And
she contemplated Gem with mingled amusement,
admiration, and dismay. " O Gem, you funny

child ! " she exclaimed, and, looking directly into his merry eyes, began to laugh heartily. Her mood was contagious. She sat upon a little mound, and Gem rolled on the grass and shouted and shrieked, and the two good comrades laughed in utter abandonment and foolish unison. There was small sense in it, perhaps, but they enjoyed it, and no "rigid wise" person was there to see or hear or condemn them.

CHAPTER X.

"O brave new world,
That has such people in it!"
—*The Tempest.*

IRCH POINT will not come to us, Gem."
"'Tain't likely."
"Then if we mean to arrive at that haven
of rest before high noon, we must bestir ourselves.
Hop up, child, and assume your half of the burden.
Would any one believe it could seem so heavy.
Lift it, Gem. This fable teaches us that we must
not loiter by the wayside and laugh till we are
weak, the next time we go on a pilgrimage with
a heavily laden basket."

She lifted the cover. "See, Gem. It is actually
full to the brim. What could have possessed me?
We might lighten our load a little. Gem, you
cannot eat all of those doughnuts, unless you have
the appetite of an anaconda, can you, now?"

"Do yer ask honest Injun, no cheatin' nor
nothin'?"

"Certainly. Perfectly 'honest Injun.'"

"Well, then, I guess if I was you, I wouldn't
throw nothin' out, except them napkins, and p'r'aps
the plates if yer want ter very bad. Cos I kalker-
late them doughnuts is pretty fair eatin'. I never
seed that ere thing yer said, an' I don't know nothin' about its appetite, but I reckon I can eat doughnuts faster'n ole Phipps can fry 'em, anyhow."

"I withdraw my objection out of respect to your powers. Not a crumb shall be wasted."

"Miss Leigh, I can carry this ere basket just as easy as stealin'. 'Tain't heavier'n nothin'. You jest let go on it. Come."

"No, sir, You will carry your half and I mine. But it was right to say that, dear, because you thought I was tired and warm. You were kind and thoughtful, Gem. Always to be so is what makes a man a gentleman."

"I s'pose he's lugged heaps o' baskets an' things for girls. He's awful kind, anyhow. Jest your sort. Real keerful-like, you know."

Leigh's attention was engrossed by a refractory glove-button.

"He gave me a reggler talkin' to cos I put a snail onto the back of Jane M'ria's neck when she was a-comin' across the barn-yard with two big pails o' milk. O, my! yer ought ter have seen her! Warn't she fun, though? She hopped, an' she yelled, and she dropped the milk, and one of the pails tipped clean over, an' marm she rowed it awful strong, an' I hid in the hen-house, an' marm got over her feelin's and then I come out. But yer'd ought to a heerd him. Didn't he give me fits, and all so quiet like, too! Don't yer never tell, hope ter die, an' I'll yer somethin'."

"I will not tell, Gem."

"He made me cry like blazes," said Jim in a shamefaced way. "Marm, she pulls my ears when she's mad, an' kin ketch me, an' she allers rows it considerable, yer know, an' I get used to it. An' dad, he don't keer much about nothin', an' lets me

alone pretty much ; an' when the marster got red
in the face and called names, I thought it was jolly
good fun ; but yer see he warn't like 'em.   No feller couldn't stan' it "—apologetically.   " He made
me cry.   He jest did.   Dead earnest and no mistake."

Perverse Leigh was interested, but not a word
would she say.

" He sot me down by the table in his room,"
continued the boy in an awe-struck voice.   " Yer
see I didn't keer about Jane M'ria, an' marm she
didn't mind nothin' except the milk bein' spilled,
and I done worser things than that to make Jane
M'ria jump, lots o' times.   But he didn't seem tc
be a-thinkin' about the milk at all."

Jimmie looked thoughtful as he went on.

" He talked kinder quiet like, yer see.   He was
a sittin' by the table too, and sometimes he looked
across at me ; but he was mostly a markin' with a
pencil, an' he warn't very long about it, neither ;
but no fellow couldn't stan' it, Miss Leigh."

" No, dear," said Leigh, softly.

" He said it was onmanly to put a snail on to
Jane M'ria.   He said as how a boy could have his
jokes.   Jokin' was good for boys.   But this was
pooty mean jokin'.   That was when he was a-begin-
nin', yer see, an' I didn't know he was a-goin'
on, an' that I couldn't stand it anyhow, an' says I,
' Well, Jane M'ria needn't go a-walkin' along with
her mouth open, and a-lookin' as if her senses had
gone off a-visitin'.   If she warn't so queer I
wouldn't 'a' wanted to put a snail on her.'

" An' he tol' me when I fit, ter fight a boy my

own size, or bigger'n me, if I wanted ter. Says I, 'Puttin' snails on ter Jane M'ria ain't fightin' any- body.' 'Yer right,' says he. 'It ain't fightin'; it's persecution, Jimmie.' He said he presumed I would'nt keer if snails crawled all over me. Says he, 'yer haven't got no nerves, Jim; but yer sister is timid an' nervous, so anything of this kind is unfair, onmanly, mean, and cruel.' Them's the words he said. Hittin' a feller when he was down, an' puttin' snails onto delicate, nervous girls, was all about the same. An' then he said I was pretty manly, an' men didn't do sech things, and he rather thought I warn't a-goin' to no more.

"An' I kinder choked up, an' that was all I said. An' says he, 'Shake hands on that Jim.' He was kinder smilin', yer see. An' somethin' or ruther made me boohoo right out. An' he said he was goin' to look up his fishin' rod, an' when he come back he asked me to go a-troutin', an' he didn't say nothin' more, yer know. We never come home till nigh sundown. Got nine: beauties they was, too. Queer what made me bawl, warn't it? He's the only feller that could 'a' made me. Couldn't stan' it, nohow. Nobody couldn't."

The child related his experience in a dramatic way that commanded Leigh's close attention. He spoke at times in unconscious imitation of Mr. Ogden's manner. Involuntarily a suspicion of amusement would creep into his tone whenever he alluded directly to that snail and the luckless Jane M'ria. He also manifested his usual faith in Mr. Ogden's infallibility, and his own tears he evidently regarded as a natural phenomenon.

" Mr. Ogden was perfectly right, Gem." Leigh felt that this approval of the enemy evinced a greatness of soul to which poor erring human nature rarely attains. "But you'll never do so any more," she said lightly. "Do you know you have been entertaining me so well the basket has grown light again? And here we are at the Point, are we not, you magnificent Gem? Take me to the cove. If I have a special desire for anything in the world, at this moment, it is for a good comfortable rock with a back to it, and cool water rippling at my feet."

Past the thickly wooded hill, through fields where were occasional clumps of poplars and pretty young birch-trees, over a rustic bridge which crossed a little winding creek, Jimmie led Miss Doane, who expressed enthusiastic delight at everything.

" Was there ever such soft velvety grass and such wavy land? The woods look lovely off there, but nothing can destroy my allegiance to the cove. The cove, my Gem, is at present my heart's desire." And soon she gained it. Nothing was wanting. The rock with a back to it, or the water rippling at her feet.

Leigh raised her umbrella. Gem threw himself on the ground and leaned against the rock. Both were silent. The low ripple of the water as the incoming tide crept nearer, the chirp of grasshoppers, and the distant note of a wood-bird, were the only sounds.

Gem, as usual, was revolving something in his mind.

" Miss Leigh, what was it yer said about them doughnuts ? "

" Doughnuts, Gem ? " with a slightly wandering air. " I'm sure I do not know. When ? "

" Yer said I couldn't eat 'em all up unless I had a appetite like a sumthin' or ruther. I never seed one. I thought I would ask yer."

" Did I say anaconda ? "

" That's the chap. What is a anaconda ? "

Leigh's features suddenly and singularly changed their expression. The air of delicious languor, the dreamy, far-off look, vanished. Thoroughly roused, with a gleam of satisfaction on her face and a wicked sparkle in her eye, she replied : —

" First class in natural history, stand up. You display a thirst for knowledge concerning the anaconda. It will afford me pleasure to impart to you my small stock of information upon this important topic. The anaconda, my dear young friend, is a snake. Its distinguishing characteristic is its capacity for swallowing anything and everything it sees. It can swallow objects morally and physically greater than itself—even as large as a young lady and her umbrella. Umbrellas do not agree with the anaconda, Gem. The anaconda belongs to the Boa family, which is spelled B-o-a, but strongly suggests B-o-r-e. Some persons, James," she added sententiously, " resemble the anaconda."

Gem eyed her curiously.

" Jokin', ain't yer ? "

" No, dear, not exactly ; but if I have given you false ideas, you can correct them when you study about snakes one of these days. I'm not wise

enough to repeat a definition from an unabridged
dictionary, but I don't like anacondas, Gem. They
take more than their share of things. Some persons are exceedingly like the anaconda. Altogether
a very disagreeable species. Ugh ! "

Having thus viciously given a Roland for Mr.
Ogden's Oliver, she felt appeased, and turned in a
jubilant way to the lunch-basket. Lunch was soon
served and soon over. Gem swallowed Miss
Phipps's dainties and Miss Doane's aphorisms apparently with equal relish, and the beauties of
nature did not materially affect the young lady's
appetite, whatever may have been her inward misgivings with regard to the propriety of having
one.

"What a lovely, long, lazy afternoon we are
going to have, Gem ! " And she settled herself com-
fortably again, after having repacked the basket,
and looked smilingly at the boy. "If our con-
sciences are clear, we ought to be perfectly happy."

"I ain't done nothin'," remarked Jim, with an
air of conscious rectitude.

"You are fortunate," said Leigh, amused, and
wondering a little about the snail and the pre-snail
period.

"I s'pose you ain't never done nothin' yer hadn't
ought ter."

The green banks of an island up the river rose
solemnly and accusingly out of the water, and stared
at guilty Leigh.

"I ? O, frequently, Gem ! Constantly, I might
say."

Gem looked incredulous. He would believe any-

thing she could tell him about long words, strange
animals, and the habits of polite society, but this
was too much.   His goddess had no human attri-
butes.   She had never put snails on people, nor
robbed orchards, nor tied saucepans to cat's tails.

Leigh knew that he was puzzled.

" My dear, I mean that I do things that are just
as naughty in me as putting snails on Jane Maria
was in you.   My snails are of a different kind, but
they are very snaily sometimes.   It is a perverse
world, Jimmie-boy, and when you and I feel like
throwing snails at people we'd better shut our teeth
together hard and run away.   If we stay where
the snails and the people are, we shall surely do
what we'll be sorry for.   All of which is a very
poor sermon.   I do not preach well, dear.   My
strongest talent, I have just discovered, lies in
lecturing upon natural history."

Chatting lazily, Leigh passed the long summer
afternoon.   It seemed singular that she had become so attached to this curious child that she did
not weary of his presence and incessant question-
ing.   She knew that a long, perfect quiet day like
this would be intolerable with an uncongenial companion.   What torture to sit upon a river-bank for
hours with a " watery smile and educated whisper,"
the typical society-man in a certain set at home,
she thought.   There are some things one must enjoy alone or with a perfectly sympathetic nature.
People who aren't responsive are so tiresome.   And
this funny little friend.   Was he responsive ? Sympathetic ?   Unquestionably.   She looked at him
earnestly, trying to fancy what manner of man he

might become. He was whistling in a pleasantly subdued way, and employing his superfluous energies in fashioning a boat, with his knife, from a piece of wood he had picked up. Gazing at the clouds and the river running by, and building air castles might do for Miss Doane. Sturdy Gem preferred whittling.

Leigh noticed the well-shaped head bent over his work, the breadth of the slightly projecting brow, the strange keenness of the deeply-set gray eyes, the flexible, refined lips. He kept them closed, too. She believed he was the only boy in Edgecomb who did not habitually go about with his mouth open. The thick mass of his bright brown hair was cut in a jagged and incomprehensible way —possibly by the maternal Holbrook's sheep-shears. His face was sunburnt and freckled and scratched ; his hands torn by brambles and rough fences. Yet, in spite of everything, he was a " bonnie, bonnie bairn."

Gem glanced up and met her intense gaze.

" What is it, Miss Leigh ? "

" What is what ? "

Gem laughed.

" I don't know exakly. Yer looks said sumthin'."

" Did they, dear ? I was wondering what I should have done down here without my Gem."

Gem's brown cheeks grew rosy with pleasure.

" If folks was like you an' he, an' if folks warn't continooally a-callin' other folks names an' a-pullin' of other folks's ears, there'd be more fun in it," he muttered.

G

Possessing the key .to Gem's enigmatical remarks, Leigh interpreted this speech as a graceful
acknowledgment of her kindness and a discreet
allusion to home-difficulties.

"Gem, wouldn't you like me to tell you a
story ? " she said, kindly. "What kind of a one
do you prefer ? "

"Most anythin', I guess, only I ain't fond of
Sunday-school books. Them pious boys allers gits
hurt or sumthin'. I ain't fond on 'em, Miss Leigh.
S'pose yer tell a bear-fightin' yarn. Make the bear
awful big, an' monstrous ugly, an' hungrier'n
nothin', cos he ain't had a scrap of a thing ter eat
fur eight days."

"What a dreadful vision, Gem ! I can almost
hear him growl. My education has been neglected,
I am afraid, for bear-hunting is Sanscrit to me.
You may tell me a bear-story some time. To-day
I will tell you something very old and sweet, that
I used to read when I was your age, and that I like
just as well now."

"Fire away. Guess I shall like it, if 'tain't
about them pious chaps what gits crushed under
wheels an' says hymns an' dies happy. I ain't fond
on 'em, yer know."

" Don't be alarmed, Gem," said Leigh, laughing.
"It is nothing of that description, I assure you.
I am afraid I know even less of such boys than of
bears."

Then she began :—

" Once upon a time, long, long ago, there was a
great, strong, beautiful, wise, good king, and he
lived far away over the sea. It was .ages ago, and

far, far away, but his country was a little like this, perhaps."

Amused at herself, yet eager to discover the resemblance, Leigh rose, and, shading her eyes with her hand, threw a long, searching look upon the surrounding landscape. North and south, east and west, she gazed, then with a satisfied air, as her glance fell on the gleaming river. "It might be flowing down to Camelot," she said. "Only a wee bit of magic, Gem, and we'd have four gray walls and four gray towers over on the island, and sleepy white lilies all around it, and the heavy barges moving slowly up and down the river, and gay little boats dancing by; and over there would be the winding road where the red-cloaked market-girls would pass, and where stately knights in shining armour would ride, and sometimes a lazy old abbot, and sometimes a dainty, graceful page. And there," pointing down the river, "would rise the towers of beautiful Camelot, the royal city. Yes, I know it was like this!" she exclaimed.

Gem calmly whittled. No person could have been more ignorant nor more indifferent than he concerning the scenery in the suburbs of Camelot, and Miss Doane might air her little poetical comparisons undisturbed by doubt or sneer.

"When this great, beautiful, wise, good king—"

"Strong," instantly corrected Gem. "You said 'strong' before, and this time you said all the rest of 'em an' left 'strong' out."

"My dear, if I were an accomplished story-teller I should know how to vary my adjectives. However, he was strong."

"How strong?"

This simple inquiry, in a business-like tone, was a wet-blanket on Leigh's enthusiasm. She did not know how strong a modern Samson ought to be in order to find favour with Gem. It was impossible for her to form any estimate of the number of pounds avoirdupois that her shadowy hero of the past had been able to lift. Puzzled, she said—

"Why, really, Gem, I do not know. He was as strong and as brave as it was possible to be."

"Bet Mr. Ogden could 'a' licked him, and done it easy, 'thout harf tryin'. Bet yer ten cents. Come, now."

"Indeed he could not," said Leigh, with indignant emphasis. "Now, Gem, you must not interrupt, please, for I have ever so much to tell, and it's growing late. When this glorious king—his name was Arthur—came to his throne, there were cruel wild men whom he had to conquer, and cruel wild beasts that he must kill." Gem stopped whittling and looked up. Thus encouraged, Leigh went on boldly. "There were bears, Gem, and dragons, and snakes, and lions, and tigers—"

"My eye!" exclaimed Gem, in ecstasy.

—"And every kind of a horrible, growling, howling, gnashing thing you can imagine. And there were maidens to be taken out of deep dark dungeons where wicked tyrants had thrown them, and castles and lands to be restored to their rightful owners, and altogether much need of the good king, and much work for him to do. And he gathered the young men of his kingdom about him, and made some lovely laws for them. And these men were brave and fierce in battle, but gentle and courteous to each other and to all women. If a man were lame, deformed in any way, they would forgive him if sometimes he were rude and ungentle in speech or manner. They thought it was a part of his infirmity. But they were so strong and brave and beautiful, they believed there was no excuse if they were not always kind and courtly to the lowliest person as to the king himself, and especially to any woman who needed aid and comfort. They thought strength should be generous to weakness, and men are stronger then women, you know, dear. Sir Launcelot was the most famous knight. In a very old book this was written of him: ' Ah ! Sir Launcelot, there thou liest that wert never matched of earthly knights' hands. Thou wert the fairest person and the goodliest of any that rode in the press of knights. Thou wert the truest friend to thy sworn brother of any that ever bestrode horse. Most courteous wert thou and gentle of all that sat in hall among dames. And thou wert the sternest knight to thy mortal foe that ever laid spear in the rest.'

" There were ever so many knights, Gem, and such lovely stories ! You will read them all some day. Only, dear, you see that they were not ashamed to do little trifling kind things for people. They forebore their own advantage. They never used rough, hard words."

Gem sat with drooping eyelids, nervously opening and shutting his knife.

" Say that again, will yer, about that chap with the spear."

Leigh again repeated " There thou liest, Sir Launcelot."

Gem's face worked queerly.

Leigh was amazed at the effect her words had produced. It was difficult even for her to realize how utterly new these ideas were to Gem. It was indeed another world opening before poor pagan Jimmie, whose ideas of right and wrong, of the wildest description, were derived from sickly narratives in which virtue was clothed in revolting colours and invariably came to some pitiful, mangled end ; and so it happened that he had dreaded holy people as one dreads disease, and never for one moment in his lawless little life had he wanted " to be an angel." There was, then, according to Miss Leigh, a theory of goodness that would not make him like stuffy old Deacon Potter, nor yet like the suffering heroes in the Sunday-school books.

" Was the little fellers like the big ones ? "

" I presume so."

Gem looked unhappy.

" What is it dear ? "

" Snails," was the laconic response.

" Gem, we will bury those snails out of sight. The knights of the Round Table would undoubtedly have put you in durance vile for that little eccentricity. But they believed that big men, and little men too, need not be naughty always because they were naughty once. And if they could see you taking such good care of a forlorn damsel far

away from friends and home, showing me the
sweetest spots in the world, bringing me ferns and
mosses when you care nothing for such things yourself, leading me so carefully over boggy places and
rough roads, amusing me, and making my days so
much less lonely and less long, and being altogether
such a faithful little squire, such a tender and true
little friend, why, Gem, they would be proud of
you, as I am. They would forgive the snail episode, provided your good sister would, and by and
by they would make a Sir Gem of you, and you
would be my knight.

Gem was more moved than he cared to show.
Still the knife-blade snapped and the little boat lay
idly by his side.

" You *are* my little knight. See ! here are my
colours." She took off her hat, untied a narrow
violet ribbon from her hair, and, quickly fashioning
it into a knot with floating ends, pinned it to the
boy's rough jacket. " The old days are gone, but
people are the same, I suppose, after all. You will
have no dragons to slay, nor anything dreadful
to do for me, but you may keep my colours, and they
say to you that I love and trust you, and believe
that you are a brave little man who is going to be
gentle as well as strong, gentle because he is strong."

A month before Gem would have looked with
impish derision upon a scene like this, and received
the colours and Leigh's little presentation-speech
with a demoniac howl. Now it all seemed right
and natural enough. It was Leigh's way of doing
things, perhaps ; or it may be Jimmie had found
his soul.

Casting a pleased look at his badge of honour, and passing his hand over it with a grimy caress, not likely to improve the delicate hue of the ribbon, he said,—

"How long did them fellers keep it up? Was they allers keerful about fightin' hard an' talkin' easy?"

"No, dear. Evil crept in among them finally."

"What became o' the smart chap?"

"Arthur was borne away to fairy-land in an enchanted barge, and—"

"He ain't the one I mean. I like t'other feller best."

"Gem, it is odd, but I always liked Launcelot better, myself. But we oughtn't. He was not nearly so good as Arthur."

"Can't help it," persisted Gem.—"I'll bet on the chap with the spear every time. He's jest like Mr. Ogden, precisely."

Leigh tried to imagine the stately Launcelot marching a luckless maiden several weary, wretched, muddy miles, and leaving her to trudge back alone as best she might, or taking a two dollar bill out of his vest pocket, or prying into a young lady's sketch-book. *He*, the anaconda, like Sir Launcelot, indeed!

Gem at that moment sprang to his feet with a spirited "By thunder! there he is!" and pranced down to the water like a mad creature. "Ship ahoy!" he shouted, making a speaking trumpet of his two hands. "Ahoy, I say! Mr. Ogden-n-n-n!" "He's put about. He's a-comin'," he said, turning and nodding encouragingly to Leigh.

She would if possible have curbed Gem's impetuous movements ; but that brilliant youth had
flashed like a meteor beyond her reach and influ·
ence before she realized his intentions.   The fatal
deed was done, Mr. Ogden summoned, and his
boat swiftly approaching, and she could only make
ready her weapons, offensive and defensive.   The
wherry turned into the cove, making for that point
on the shore where a small figure was capering
about wildly, and sending characteristic shouts of
welcome over the water.

" Ain't she a beauty !   Ain't she a bird ! Here's
me, an' here's her, an' here's every blessed one of
us."

Philip brought the boat plumply up on the shore.
Turning his head just enough to see the inimitable
Jim, but not sufficiently to command a view of that
dignified young person who stood with an air of
elegant unconcern farther up the bank, he said carelessly, " Jump in, old fellow," never dreaming but
that Jim was alone, and that he wished to avail
himself of the opportunity of a row home.   Blind
and obtuse man, who had caught but a part of the
child's remarks, and fancied " here's her " referred
to the wherry.

" O, come now, take her !   She ain't a mite
afraid.   She'd like to go first-rate, wouldn't yer,
Miss Leigh."

" No, I thank you, Gem, not to-night, if you
please," " a voice replied far up the height,"—a
voice which sounded mischievous in spite of itself,
and which gave Mr. Ogden his first intimation of the
presence of a third person.   Surprised, he turned

quickly, and saw Miss Doane leaning in assumed
nonchalance against a great rock. In her hand was
the famous umbrella, which, like the " snow-white
plume " of King Henry of Navarre, was always in
the thickest of the fight. The low light from the
western sky behind her, shining through her pretty
hair, made a golden halo round a head which, it
is evident, was not that of a saint.

He was for an instant thrown off his guard.
Leigh saw it with wicked joy.

"I beg a thousand pardons, Miss Doane. I did
not see you until this moment."

"That is not of the slightest consequence, Mr.
Ogden," she returned with ineffable dignity, putting on her hat, and throwing her shawl over her
shoulders.

"Gem, are you coming with me, or do you prefer to row back?" she calmly inquired.

Gem looked blank.

> "A child may say ' Amen '
> To a bishop's prayer, and see the way it goes ";

and Gem, though all unused to the inscrutable
ways of society, and to the method by which young
ladies and gentlemen ceremoniously scratch out
one another's eyes, could yet perceive that a heavy
cloud hung gloomily between his two bright particular stars.

Looking with disappointed, wondering eyes from
his beloved boatman to Leigh, he said sadly,—

"I brung yer here, an' I'll see yer home ; but if
yer'd only just get into this wherry an'—"

" Come, dear," said Leigh impressively. "It is growing very late."

She felt that at last her star was in the ascendant. While the enemy, unconscious of her presence, had drawn up to the shore and sat with back turned and unconscious mien, she had had time to observe the ludicrous elements of the scene as well as to prepare for battle. This temporary advantage she fully appreciated, and, together with poor Jim's bewilderment and comical chagrin, it had the effect of somewhat diminishing the resentment she had previously cherished towards Mr. Ogden. Still, it was with a superb and lofty air that she condescended to make a slight inclination in the direction of the boat, and a most majestic " Good evening, Mr. Ogden," that she deigned to bestow upon him.

" Good evening, Miss Doane," was the stiff response. "Come up to my room when you get back, will you, Jim."

" All right," said the boy, subdued beyond belief.

The two figures climbing the bank, as before swinging the basket, stood boldly out in the mellow sunset light.

Philip could hear their voices, and the free, merry laugh with which Leigh greeted some of Gem's philosophy.

" The vials of her wrath she delights to empty on my head ; while to my friend Jim she is all softness and sunshine. She honoured me this evening by calling me by my name, which is more than she deigned to do at our last interview of

refrigerator memory.   Yet, 'To err is feminine,
to forgive impossible,' is no doubt her motto.
Did Edgecomb throw a glamour over her, or had
she *in propria persona* that picturesque, wood-
nymph look?   How she manages to start up suddenly out of the ground and make a picture of
herself!" he thought, recalling her attitude as she
stood with her hat in her hand, her lovely face
slightly flushed by her long day of wandering, and
her shining hair roughened by little breezes.
Likening her to the Lorelei, and feeling like begging his own pardon for so execrable a pun, he
pulled with strong, steady stroke out of the cove
and up the river.

CHAPTER XI.

"The gentler-born the maiden, the more bound,
My father, to be sweet and serviceable
To noble knights in sickness, as you know,
When these have worn their tokens."
—ELAINE.

"ROBERT, Robert, toi que j'aime," sang Leigh, with operatic abandon, as she dusted her books, arranged a few flowers, and shook her table-cover vigorously out of a window.

Loud and clear and happy sounded her morning-carol to Philip Ogden's ears as he passed under the elms and up the old-fashioned paved walk that led from the gate to the door. Wide open were the three windows of the girl's room. In came the sunshine and light morning breeze, and out went the flood of melody. More extravagant and audacious grew the singer every moment, until, after improvising a marvellous cadenza, the like of which was never attempted upon any known stage, and executing what might be called an impossible trill, she concluded her efforts with a defiant little shriek on the highest note she could reach, and stopped to regain her breath. And Philip, standing down at the porch, feeling like a wretched intruder, or as if he had been again discovered gazing in her sketch-book, knowing well that he was the last person in the world whom Miss Doane would

have selected to represent an enraptured audience, thought that a kindred impulse to that
which made Jim stand on his head and turn
handsprings was animating the many-sided young
lady.

The sunshine and warmth, her sweet fresh youth
and health, and a dash of childlike fun, were all
expressed in the glad notes she poured forth with
such delicious freedom as she moved about her
room. The gentlemanly anaconda, following the
instincts of his nature, swallowed the happy tones
and the picture they suggested.

The girl's voice sounded childlike and innocent.
He was sorry when she stopped. He liked to hear
her, as one likes anything joyful and fresh and free.
The chameleon had never before presented to his
gaze so attractive a hue.

Not wishing to deliberately put himself in the
way of meeting Miss Doane, he had come there that
morning most unwillingly, and only because he
could not in kindness refuse. Now, he was not
sorry. He was quite unused to girls and their
little home-ways, and he felt kindly and cordially,
for the moment, to this girl of the happy voice with
the "fun" in it, who busied herself about her
room and sang in the morning sunshine for pure
gladness of heart. He was grateful for the glimpse
she had all unconsciously given him of her real
self, although he knew it was highly probable that
she would clothe herself with pride as with a gar-
ment, and descend that quaint old staircase with
all the majesty of a line of kings.

"Robert, Robert," began the girl with renewed
energy.

Philip had knocked once, and patiently waited for somebody to appear.

No one came.

Bees buzzed about the honeysuckles by the porch, the fragrance of sweet-peas and great white lilies stole round pleasantly from the garden at the side of the house, the sun shone in through the open door on the faded oil-cloth, and above, Leigh was attempting another extravaganza. He ventured once more to raise the heavy knocker. Leigh, deeply absorbed, heard nothing but her own voice, of which the volume of tone was no slight thing.

Miss Phipps at last opened a door at the end of the hall and peered out curiously.

" Oh ! " she said, advancing. " My hands was in the dough, an' I didn't know but she was round somewheres. Oh ! You're the one as was here before, ain't yer ? Be yer any relation o' hern ? "

" I have not that honour," said the young man, amiably. " Will you be kind enough to give this to Miss Doane ? " extending his card.

Miss Phipps slowly drew her spectacle-case from her pocket, the spectacles from the case, and, as on the previous occasion when Mr. Ogden had appeared at her door, subjected him and his card to a severe scrutiny, which he bore unflinchingly.

" That's her up there a-hollerin." Having communicated the self-evident fact, she added : " She allers screeches mornin's when she's a-fixin' her flowers. Thought she'd make me deef when she first come. Used to it now. Like to hear her goin's-on. Sounds kinder cheerful like, don't it now ? " And a smile actually hovered for a moment over her grim features.

Philip civilly said "Very," and mildly renewed his suggestion that his card should be presented to the attic warbler.

Whereupon Miss Phipps shouts from the foot of the stairs, with force sufficient to interrupt Leigh in one of her most elaborate and impassioned flights.

"Yes, Miss Phipps, what is it?" comes pleasantly down in her ordinary voice.

It does not occur to her to move from her apartments, knowing the usual tenor of Phipps's remarks. Does she want the apple-pies sweetened with sugar, or molasses, and will she have caraway-seeds in the cookies, or something of similar import, Leigh expects to be asked.

Instead, distinct and shrill from the foot of the stairs ascend these ominous words,—

"Mr. Phillup Ogdin"—"*O*-gden" she called it, reading from the card, and suggesting "ogre" to her listeners—"is a waitin' down here to see yer."

Gone are the merry roulades, and "all the air a solemn stillness holds."

The silence above can be felt.

Below, the ancient Phipps remarks audibly,—

"Her door's open. She's up there, an' she's heerd. I don' know why she don't answer, but I s'pose she'll come down when she gits ready." With which eminently cheering and sagacious announcement, after inviting Philip to come in an' take a cheer," and imparting the valuable information that "sittin's as cheap as standin," her tall, gaunt figure vanishes from his gaze, and she goes where her dough awaits her.

Presently Leigh, with lady-like composure, comes down the broad staircase. Certainly no mortal could accuse that demure damsel of ever raising her voice above regulation rules, and shouting for joy.

She realized that he must have heard her musical uproar, and had wished somewhat impatiently that once in a while he might appear in an ordinary fashion, if it were, as it seemed to be, an unalterable decree of fate that she and " that man " must meet. Having only taken sufficient time to assume, as photographers say, the expression she wished to wear, she appeared before Philip, feeling as if she were acting a prominent part in a genteel comedy.

The expression was well chosen. It conveyed no idea of her wonder as to his object in coming, nor yet of her strong desire to laugh out frankly because she had been discovered making the morning hideous.

Not the faintest hint that he had heard anything which he was not expected to hear appeared on his countenance, as he responded to her " Good morning."

" I am sorry to disturb you so early, Miss Doane, but Jimmie sent me. I come at his urgent request. As the little fellow's ill, I could not refuse."

" Gem ill ! " she exclaimed. " Is it possible ! Is he very ill ? " she asked, anxiously forgetting that she was talking to the anaconda, and must remember her dignity. Frankly the great brown eyes, full of sympathy for her little friend, looked down at him as he stood on a lower step.

H

" They call it a low fever.   He is not seriously ill
at present, but I presume he may become so.   He
seems weak and listless, and once in a while his
mind wanders a little.   The people at the cottage
arn't used to sickness, and don't make the boy
any too happy, and this morning he begged so
piteously to see you, that I could do no less than
tell you."

" O, certainly ! " Leigh said.   " Poor little Gem !
I will go at once."

" I have a waggon out here," began Philip.

" And you are going to drive me down ?   That
will be ever so much better than walking," Leigh
said hurriedly."   "I will be ready in a very few
moments."   And she ran rapidly up to her room.

Not a vestige of her former wrath appeared, yet
Philip could not flatter himself that he personally
had in the remotest degree caused this change of
manner, which was nevertheless welcome.   No man
of tolerably good intentions enjoys being treated as
an obnoxious, hardened sinner by a young and
pretty woman.   And Philip was pleased that the
happy, singing girl had not been transformed, by
the sight of him, into that incomprehensible being
whose frigid majesty of deportment he vividly recalled.

Leigh soon appeared with her hat on, and a small
travelling-bag in her hand.   She had changed her
morning robe for the memorable brown dress she
had worn at the fort.   He fancied the old manner
must of necessity accompany it, the two were so
closely allied in his mental photograph of her, and
was relieved that he saw no indications of an imme-
diate relapse.

" I am sorry to put you into this jolting vehi-cle," he said, as they passed down the walk. " It is the best the Holbrook stables afford."

" How long has he been ill ? " And Leigh stepped into the old waggon with an abstracted air. " I have not seen him in three days. Has he been ill so long ? "

Philip, amused, decided that the sooner he real-ized that he was a nonentity the better. Except that he could answer questions about Gem, he ap-parently had no more existence in Miss Doane's mind than if he were an automaton driver. It occurred to him that her former treatment of him was, upon the whole, more flattering ; yet, not be-ing inordinately vain, he enjoyed playing "dummy." The girl's simplicity of manner and directness of purpose pleased him, and altogether he found her a curious study.

" I believe it was the day after he was at Birch Point with you, Miss Doane, that he complained of his head. He had been indulging in what the doctor called an intemperate use of water. The boy swims like a fish, and has been in the river oftener than usual of late, and remained in too long. It's too far north for much of that sort of thing."

Leigh said nothing. Philip glanced at her as they bounced and jolted along. All in quiet brown, with a thoughtful look on her face, the Puritan maiden Priscilla could not have seemed more sweet and staid. The hot sun was pouring down upon her ungloved hands. They were white and small and ringless, he saw.

Man-like, he thoughtlessly said exactly the wrong thing.

"This is a broiling sun. It is a pity you did not bring your umbrella"; and instantly could have bitten his tongue out for his maladroit speech.

Leigh coloured to her temples. Her umbrella ! Once upon a time, ages upon ages ago, she and this man had climbed that very hill together. If this fact had occurred to her during the drive, it had been in a vague, shadowy way. All her vexation and dislike, her extravagant denunciations of him, had seemed so far off and unimportant. Sympathy for Gem had outweighed everything else. But that fatal umbrella ! Again had it thrust itself forward and done an evil deed.

She did not know whether his remark was intentional or not, but she felt disturbed, and fully conscious of the unpleasant past.

She made an effort to speak amiably. She was not ungenerous enough to wish to be less than gracious to the enemy who plainly admitted that he was acting as her escort solely at the request of a sick child, but the voice that replied, "The sun does not trouble me in the least, and we shall soon be there," was not the caressing voice of the girl who walked off swinging the basket and chatting with Gem in the sunset light at Birch Point, nor yet the careless, merry voice of the singer, nor that of the calm and thoughtful Puritan maiden. It was, it must be confessed, painfully conventional, and remotely suggestive of the atmosphere of the Arctic regions.

Both felt ill at ease, and silently congratulated

themselves that the beauty of the raw-boned nag, which cheerfully and clumsily galloped up and down the hills, was surpassed by his speed.

Philip ushered Leigh into the ponderous presence of Mrs. [Holbrook, who, not being in the habit of devoting much time to the amenities of life, did not thank the young lady for coming.   Giving her a hard stare, she remarked—

" Jim allers was onthrifty.   Never had no sense.   An' now ef he ain't gone an' chosen the most on-convenient season to up an' be sick in, right in the midst of the hayin', an' me to my ears in raspberry jam."

Philip perceived that Leigh must have had some previous knowledge of the idiosyncrasies of Jim-mie's mamma.   The young lady did not manifest the faintest surprise at the tender motherliness of Mrs. Holbrook's sentiments, but quietly said that she had no doubt Mrs. Holbrook was extremely busy, and she should be glad to relieve her of the care of Jimmie for a while, and might she go to him.

Her manner was, as it needed to be, the perfec-tion of tact, for she had come to beard the Hol-brook in her den.

Preceded by the sorrowing mother, followed by Philip, with the shrinking Jane Maria bringing up the rear of the procession, Leigh entered the large cheerless room on the first floor, where Gem lay. He usually occupied a loft in the roof, but the air up there was so stifling, Philip had offered an in-tercessory prayer to the grim deity who ruled the household, and had succeeded in inducing her to allow him to bring the child down where he at least would not die of suffocation.

She had no intention of being inhuman, but her manner from the beginning of Gem's illness had given Philip a savage desire to shake her, although he told himself he might as well attempt to shake Mount Washington. Had her youth been such a "demd horrid grind," he wondered, that it had crushed every possibility of kindly sympathy out of her nature! She made no special effort to worry the boy. She had a natural aptitude for making people miserable, and her invincible obtuseness in this respect was her stronghold. When what Philip termed her "nagging" was more than usually intense, in pity he would devise some means of sending her from the room, and had befriended the boy in many ways. Mrs. Holbrook saw no necessity of consulting a physician, until Philip urged it upon her. When the doctor had made his visit, pronounced Jimmie veritably ill, with danger of congestion of the brain, prescribed his remedies, and departed, then arose that formidable woman, not wishing to be outdone in her own house, and threatened the invalid with a heavy dose of castor-oil, which was to be followed at once, she volubly declared, by a large bowl of saffron tea. Moved to desperation by Jimmie's horror-struck, disgusted face, as she came towards the bed with the castor-oil bottle in one hand and brandishing a huge pewter spoon in the other, a forcible counterpart of the immortal Mrs. Squeers, the young man sprang to his feet and exclaimed, "My dear Mrs. Holbrook, is it—can it be—your jam burning? Let *me* give

that to Jimmie." And, looking profoundly anxious
to assist her, he took from her hand the imple-
ments of torture. Telling him the tea was all
ready on the mantel-piece, she withdrew, uttering
violent imprecations upon "Jane M'ria's shiftless-
ness." Whereupon the arch hypocrite surprised
the hollyhocks growing just outside the window
with a liberal deluge of castor-oil and saffron tea.
When she returned, he gave her the bottle, in
which the oil was perceptibly lower, and unblushingly stated that "the saffron tea went down very
well, and he thought Jim enjoyed it," suspect-
ing the latter remark would prevent her from bringing in a fresh supply. He piously hoped the re-
cording angel would treat this righteous fraud as
leniently as he did Uncle Toby's oath, and that the
deceitful deed performed deliberately before Jim's
grateful eyes might not have a fatal effect upon
that youth's subsequent career.

It had seemed to Philip that the boy was very
ill. At times he would lie almost in a stupor,
wanting nothing, saying nothing ; then would sleep
a few moments, and upon waking would talk inco-
herently. Whenever he seemed sufficiently roused
to speak rationally, he would implore Philip to ask
Miss Leigh to come.

"She likes me first-rate," he confidently asserted.
"She will come. I know she will."

This morning especially he had begged so hard
for her, that Philip put his pride in his pocket,
harnessed a horse himself, and did as the child
desired. Mr Holbrook, a spiritless, dejected man,
was out in a field not far from the house. Philip

knew that he would have gone, but thought it
useless to disturb him. The young man always
treated the farmer with the most respectful courtesy. A man who had endured twenty years'
companionship with such a spouse, and had *lived*,
was a martyr pure and simple. No wonder his
eyes looked dazed and weary, and that he rarely
spoke.

To Edgecomb proper then Philip had gone to
please the boy ; and before he had seen Leigh he
had an interview with the doctor, wishing to ascertain that the fever was not of a contagious character. This he felt bound to do on Tom's account,
the young lady being still, as he told himself with
a curious smile, under his guardian care. " Docile
little creature ! How pleased she will be to see
me ! " he thought, as his awkward Dobbin stopped
at Miss Phipps's. But Leigh had not bestowed
upon him the anticipated stony stare, nor had she
treated him in any respect as an outlaw. She
had come willingly, eagerly, to the little boy who
needed her so sorely ; and now Philip stood watching her as she quietly took off her hat, laid it on
a chair, and leaned tenderly over the flushed little
face. She passed one arm under Gem's shoulders,
lifting him easily, quickly shook his pillow and
turned it. The commonplace deed excited Philip's
admiration. He had once seen a similar thing done
upon the stage, and had thought it a very pretty
piece of acting.

From Leigh's pleasant ways his attention was
suddenly diverted by Mrs. Holbrook, who, with
her usual appreciation of the eternal fitness of

things, took this favourable opportunity to explore the long-neglected closet of this unused room. From its cavernous depths she exhumed boxes, bags, and old clothes, accompanied by clouds of dust and torrents of words. Not content with opening and shutting drawers with a prodigious noise, she procured a hammer, with the laudable intention of improving the shining hour by driving a few nails.

The effect upon Gem, and also upon Leigh and Philip, through sympathy, was maddening. Gem tossed and turned uneasily. Leigh glanced over her shoulder at Philip, then threw a comical look of abhorrence at the closet-door ; and each felt, as the pounding waxed more and more furious, that the moment had arrived when patience ceased to be a virtue—yet what could they do? There was no law that forbade a woman to drive as many nails as she pleased in her own house. Gem groaned, and looked half frantic. Leigh rapidly crossed the room to Philip, who was standing on the threshold waiting to see if he could be of any use, and in an undertone, yet in a decided, impetuous fashion, said—

" Do try to make that impossible woman go away and stay away."

" I'll do my best," muttered Philip. " I'd like to choke her," he added savagely. Leigh gave an approving and sympathetic nod, which plainly intimated that she would hugely enjoy acting as his assistant, should he carry his barbarous wish into execution. Thus was tacitly formed a society for the suppression of the Holbrook. The grievances and quarrels of their own mighty feud they ignored, uniting against the common enemy for the good of the child. The anti-Holbrook League was an unpremeditated thing—the result of a word and a glance—yet it was made in good faith, and would last just so long as Gem's pitiful case necessitated the strange alliance. Silently, gracefully, they buried the hatchet. There would be time enough in future, should occasion demand, to assume fresh war-paint and renew hostilities.

Leigh returned to Gem. The pounding continued.

Philip reasoned that no *ruse de guerre* would be of use in this emergency, and then, indeed, it would have been difficult for him to invent one. He had already availed himself of and exhausted the "jam." What, then, remained, he anxiously asked himself. Plainly, nothing but brute force or moral suasion. Everybody always yielded to the Holbrook. Might not deliberate disapproval and opposition prove a successful experiment as an entire novelty? She might, it is true, grow exceeding irate, and request him to change his boarding-place, which result he should deeply deplore, on Jimmie's account. Still, he was aware that his board was an agreeable increase of revenue of which it was not probable that she would wish to deprive herself.

"This will not do, Mrs. Holbrook," he said. "You must let these things alone to-day, and arrange them when Jim is well. You'll kill the boy with so much noise. Miss Doane is kind enough to sit with him for a while, and when she is weary I will be happy to take her place. We are willing to relieve you as much as possible of the care of him, but I must insist upon quiet in the room, or no one can answer for the consequences. There are too many here. Perhaps you and I had better go out."

All of which Philip uttered in an emphatic tone of masculine authority, with the air of one who has never had his will crossed, nor dreams that such a possibility exists. The tyrant and termagant mechanically pushed back into the closet the *débris* she had scattered over the floor. She then ejaculated a stupefied " Well, I never !" and turned and glared suspiciously at Leigh. That discreet young person, however, wore the most innocent and unconscious air in the world, as she stood with averted face, and apparently never a thought beyond Gem. Philip, talking incessantly, in order to steal Mrs. Holbrook's thunder and not lose a point he had gained, conveyed the nonplussed woman into the kitchen.

As he closed the door of Gem's room, Leigh smiled and nodded in friendly farewell, while the brown eyes looked both amused and grateful.

The perfect quiet in the room after the exhausting noise and confusion, seemed grateful to Gem, who lay motionless for a little time.

" Who brung yer letters ? I wanted ter. Couldn't, though," he murmured sorrowfully, as if he had betrayed a trust.

" My child, don't think of them for a moment. I'm going to bathe your head. Shut your eyes, and you may drop off into a pleasant little nap."

"When I wake up will you be right there a-lookin' at me?"

"Yes, dear."

Gem smiled, and closed his eyes.

He dozed a few moments, then started up wildly and clung to Leigh.

"What is it, little one?"

"I thought you was gone. Marm was a-pullin' yer off."

"You dreamed it, dear," she said, softly. "I came to take care of you, and I promise you I will stay. Do not be afraid. No one will take me away from you."

"Yer're awful good," whispered the boy. "What makes yer?"

"What makes me good to you? Because you are my precious little Gem, and my knight, you know."

Full of regret at seeing her merry little comrade lying ill before her, pitying the sick child who seemed worse than motherless, loving him more than ever before because he appealed so strongly to her warm womanly sympathies, she stooped and touched his forehead with her lips, saying, softly,—

"Be quiet, dear. You may sleep again. I will not leave you."

"Deep into Gem's heart sank the tender caress. Again he closed his eyes, and soon fell into a restless, nervous sleep.

And Leigh sat watching him, and soothing him when he would wake, by her calm and sweet presence, and low, loving voice.

Beyond the closed door, Philip, in the hot kitchen, was throwing sops to Cerberus.

CHAPTER XII.

" "It is best to begin with a little aversion."
—MRS. MALAPROP.

"PARDON me, Miss Doane, but why should you ? "

" Pardon me, Mr. Ogden, but why should I not ? "

Standing out in the cottage-porch, they looked steadily at each other in the soft summer twilight. Already there were symptoms of dissension within the newly-formed League. Upon Leigh's face was determination ; upon Philip's disapproval.

" I may take a liberty in expressing my opinion," said Philip, somewhat stiffly, " but if you will permit me to speak plainly, I see no reason why you should give yourself so much unnecessary trouble."

" Gem wants me."

" I presume he does. It is not surprising that he should. Florence Nightingales do not abound in this family. Still Jim and I don't quarrel much, and if you will resign him to me for to-night, I will agree to call at Miss Phipps's for you to-morrow morning at any unearthly hour you will indicate."

" You are very kind, but Gem wants me," reiterated Leigh, as if that simple fact settled the matter.

Philip, with concealed impatience, wondered at the unreasoning feminine persistence he was encountering. That he was equally persistent did not, of course, occur to him.

"Ought you to stay, Miss Doane? It is very benevolent in you, no doubt, but—pardon me—is it not also rather Quixotic? Jim is in no danger; my bungling ministrations to-night, though a painful contrast to yours, won't kill him, and I can shield him from the attacks of the harpy. You had better allow me to take you back. It seems unwise for you to run any risk entirely alone, and away from your friends. The child is in reality nothing to you."

"The child is in reality my friend," said Leigh, quickly and decidedly; "and when I left my family behind me, I did not also leave my judgment, nor my ordinary human instincts."

"Nor your own sweet will," thought Philip.

"I do not see that the matter admits of any further discussion, Mr. Ogden. Gem is my friend, and needs me."

"A remarkably fine sentiment," was Philip's mental comment. Aloud, he said dryly,—

"Your friendship, Miss Doane, must be a more substantial and valuable thing than that of most young women—according to books."

"That may be," she coolly retorted; "yet allow me to say, Mr. Ogden, that if you have derived your ideas on the subject from books only, it is possible that you have not the faintest conception what a good, honest, and substantial thing a young woman's friendship really is." Here the manner of the spirited champion of her sex suddenly changed, and with a bright smile and a frankly extended hand she said, "But I cannot afford to quarrel with you, Mr. Ogden. You deserve a martyr's crown for your efforts to day. All day long with that woman!" she exclaimed with an expressive shudder. "I really did not know a *man*"—with a slight saucy emphasis—"could be so unselfish. Please let me stay." And she looked up sweetly at the amazed young man, like an imploring child.

"Please let her stay!" Had the skies fallen? And was there anything in the world so swift and subtle as a woman's wit? He was grave and displeased, and like lightning she had changed her tactics for Gem's sake. They two for Gem, and Philip against the household, was their united battle cry, while her little private watchword was, "For Gem's sake." Plainly she had said that she could not afford to quarrel with him. His friendliness was necessary to the success of her present plans ; and now she stood, meek and dutiful, with appealing eyes, knowing instinctively it was the surest method of banishing the slight frown which she herself had produced upon Philip's face. Yet her art was so palpable, so childlike, so intentionally and honestly revealed, that Philip, perfectly appreciating the workings of her mind, smiled down upon her kindly ; then, with affected solemnity, said :

"Miss Doane, if you have gained your ideas of man's selfishness from books simply, it is possible that you have not the faintest conception what a noble, grand, heroic, and utterly unselfish creature he really is."

" You are quite right. I do not think I have,"
said Leigh, laughing ; " but if you will be good
enough to bring me a sheet of paper and a pencil,
and kindly take a note to Miss Phipps, you may,
perhaps, do much towards convincing me."

" I am entirely at your service. I will take you
or your note to Miss Phipps, as you finally decide ;
but, for the last time, allow me to beg you to leave
Jim to me to-night." He spoke earnestly and
kindly.

She replied, " Please say no more about it, Mr.
Ogden. You will oblige me very much by taking
the note."

He silently bowed, and went to his room for writing materials. " Is there anything else that I can
do ? " he said, as he took the note from Leigh's
hand, and was about to turn towards the gate,
where he had left the waggon.

" Nothing, thank you, except not to let Mrs. Holbrook drive me away," she whispered roguishly.
And Philip, as self-installed keeper and tamer of
that ferocious person, pledged his word to Leigh
that she should not be molested.

" Shall I bring your letters ? I shall go to the
post-office."

" Thank you ; you may bring them to-night, and,
if not too much trouble, whenever I am here. The
post-office is the least agreeable place in Edg-
comb."

" Yes, I know. It is where the loafers most do
congregate, though they are, as a rule, such Rip
Van Winkles, they are quite harmless. It will be
no trouble to me, Miss Doane. I consider it an
honour to act as your postman."

With an amicable good-evening, they parted. Again Philip turned back, and, approaching the cottage-door, said :

"I may not see you this evening when I get back. If you need any help to-night you will not hesitate to call me. You might get frightened or distressed, you know, and we can't afford to quarrel, as you say, or be too conventional just at present. You may command me to an unlimited extent—for the boy's sake," he added, with a twinkle in his eye.

"I probably shall not need to disturb you, as I am not at all timid ; but I promise to hesitate at nothing—for Gem's sake," she added, smiling mischievously.

Soon the waggon jolted out of sight. Leigh stood looking out upon the dusky landscape. The faint outline of distant hills, the intense gloom of nearer forests, her conversation with Philip, and his calm, direct gaze, the strong, salt breeze that was blowing her hair back from her temples as she leaned against the lattice of the porch a few moments before returning to her little charge, all seemed familiar as a twice-told tale. "Why, this is the way girls in books feel," she thought. "They always have lived through certain moments ages before, and everything is like a scene long past. Such nonsensical romantic sensations will never do for me." And she gave a funny little shrug, and tried to shake off the impression. What was Bessie doing ? Would Mr. Ogden bring her a letter, she wondered. What unaccountable things one's prejudices were ? She half admitted that she did

I

not really dislike him so much as she ought, in reason. She did not like him. She never should. If there was anything she could trust in the world, it was her intuition, and that unerring guide had pronounced against him. The fiat had gone forth. They were not sympathetic. Still, she must in justice grant that he had been really kind that day. Keeping faithful guard over the Holbrook all day long in that hot kitchen was a sacrifice, when a man might be wandering off with his fishing-rod, or skimming down the river in his wherry. He had done nothing that would reflect any credit upon him in the eyes of people in general, but she liked it in him, it was so purely kind. And then, with a brief spasm of contrition, she asked herself if she ought to express her regret for the combined misdemeanours of her unruly umbrella and more unruly self. She involuntarily recoiled at the idea. Ah, no ! she had felt so strongly; she could not yet speak of those things that had passed away. The new and the old Mr. Ogden were two individuals, one little day had proved such a peacemaker. But how could she tell what freak would seize her if she should try to make any allusion to the disastrous opening of their acquaintance, what perverse fancy would transform the young man whose manner was so friendly to her, so thoughtful for Gem, into the self-satisfied anaconda, pervading space in every direction, and constantly rearing his hateful head before her unwilling eyes ? No, she could not trust herself. She was too capricious. Things might remain as they were, and when Tom and Bessie came she might dare, reinforced so strongly, to ask

Mr. Ogden's pardon once for all for whatever hei-
nous offences she had committed; and then her conscience—whose demands were not very clamorous
on that point—would be appeased, and Mr. Ogden
would depart, and her summer's experience would
be only an episode for Bessie and herself to talk
over, and that would be the end of it. But surely
now she need not precipitate matters, stir the
peaceful waters until once more they would become turbid. The truth was, they were not friends.
But she assured herself, with lofty pride, her mind
was not so narrow as to refuse to recognise ob-
vious admirable traits, even in an enemy. He had
been kind, useful, unselfish, and that was more
than men usually took the trouble to be, this experienced observer of the race concluded. And
his face was not disagreeable when he looked that
way, she mused. "That way," the expression of
which it had pleased Leigh to approve, was the one
which had accompanied Philip's final offer of assistance, the look of kindly amusement with which
he had told her to command him for the boy's sake.
Immediately, as if some one had accused her of
deserting her principles, she told herself with considerable asperity that she presumed even if she did
not fancy a man's prominent mental characteristics,
that fact ought not to prevent her from acknow-
ledging that his eyes had a pleasant twinkle, that
the lines of his face were strong and shrewd, that
his head was well set on a pair of broad shoulders,
and that he had extremely good manners. No!
she hoped, into whatever fault she might fall
through the infirmities of her nature, that she

should never grow so illiberal as to distort facts,
simply from her own private prejudice.   Then the
enviable possessor of this superhumanly clear and
unbiassed judgment ;turned from the starlight and
the cool breeze and returned to her post determin-
ing that while she remained in the Holbrook cottage she would vigorously wave her flag of truce
in Mr. Ogden's face, "for Gem's sake," as she re-
peatedly assured herself.

Through the woods rode Philip to do Leigh's
bidding, pondering pleasantly, for the first time,
upon the many phases her nature had exhibited.
Which aspect showed the girl's true self ?   Which
manner was the abnormal one ?   He laughingly
admitted that he knew not; but that she was
bright and bewitching, and extremely fond of her
own way, was the latest impression he had formed.
What new role it might please her to assume in
the morning was beyond surmise.   "Colours seen
by candlelight do not look the same by day."   But
this he resolved, that while he would be her most
faithful servant and ally in every matter wherein
Jim was directly or remotely concerned, he would
be careful not to presume upon the familiar and
friendly relations so established.   Until Miss Doane
made it evident that he was personally, and not
"for Gem's sake," entitled to ordinary amicable
treatment, he would studiously avoid infringing
upon her divine right to be let alone, which she
had clearly proclaimed to him.   Their present
"platform" was good for this day only, or at
least for Jim's illness ; and when the hollow and
unsubstantial thing should vanish in thin air, it

was possible Miss Doane's smiles would also take to themselves wings; it therefore was fitting that a wise man should be prudent, and consider his ways, and not put his trust in a treaty of peace of a manifestly ephemeral nature, and made by a beautiful kaleidoscopic young woman. "She can be charming and sunny as the day; but if she be not so to me for my own merits, what care I how transcendentally agreeable she be!" he coolly thought. And then he vowed a solemn vow. Miss Doane should allude to their woful encounter, or never should the matter cross his lips; and she should first express one little word of regret for her reception of him at the fort, or he would never ask her pardon for his various delinquencies. If she would take one step towards him in honest apology, he would be willing to walk miles to meet her, he knew well; but she must make the first advance. Once he had begun in good faith to express his contrition, and she had repulsed him. Now he would be passive, and await some active demonstration from her. So he buckled on his armour of obstinacy, because, though he did not admit it, he was in peril from the unconscious attacks of the plausible, sweet-voiced, friendly enemy who had stood talking with him in the porch.

Later, when he returned, and had put up his horse, and walked in at the back door, with the freedom and independence of a son of the soil, he found a maiden all forlorn crouching disconsolately upon a low stool by the cold kitchen stove. The light was dim, but the length and prominence of the elbows revealed Jane Maria. She was sobbing, and evidently in much distress. Too frequently had Philip seen her in grief to be amazed, and he ventured a word of comfort to the ungainly likeness of Cinderella mourning amid the ashes of the desolate hearthstone.

"'Tears, idle tears!' Miss Jennie; and what was it to-day? What have you done that you ought not to have done, or not done that you ought to have done, and has the mother been remonstrating?" he asked lightly.

"No, sir, 't ain't that, it's Jimmie."

"So? And what can the boy have done to tease you in his present condition?"

"No, sir, 't ain't that. I wish he hed," she said with a fresh burst of tears.

It had become Philip's destiny of late to observe more clearly than ever before the complex workings of the feminine nature. He flattered himself that he was beginning to be hardened to Miss Doane's "bewilderingly various combinations," to quote from the eloquent advertisements of the sensational plays; but that Jane Maria's silly, simple little mind should develop in any unexpected way was indeed a surprise.

"Suppose you try to stop crying and take this package to Miss Doane, tell her there were no letters for her, and ask her how Jim seems."

She went obediently, and returned with Miss Doane's thanks for Mr. Ogden, and Jimmie seemed restless and nervous and full of pain, but she hoped to be able to quiet him.

"I hope she will," said Philip, heartily. "And now, Miss Jennie, tell me why you feel so distressed about him."

"Cos he spoke so pleasant-like to the young lady, and cos his back and his head hurts him, and cos he ain't said nothin' about my elbows sence he was sick."

"Ah, I see! And you think these symptoms so unnatural that you feel alarmed,—afraid he won't recover."

"I was afraid he was a-repentin', and they most allers repents just before they dies, and nobody ever died here and I don't want Jimmie ter." And the poor girl sobbed convulsively.

Her grief though ludicrous, was heartfelt.

"But he will not," said Philip confidently. "Don't shed another tear for him. He has not repented enough to hurt himself, and will live to torment you many a long year."

This charming prospect consoled her immensely. She could not doubt, for Philip had spoken.

"It seems, then, that you are fond of the boy, Miss Jennie?"

She looked up doubtfully. "I don' know. I ain't fond of him when he calls me names, and jumps at me in the dark. He ain't a bit like the Lady I-mer-gin's little brother. He was tall an' pale an' had long curls, and wore a black velvet cloak lined with crimson satin, and he used to say, 'What ho! Without there! Hither, minion!'"

"Jim could say that without any difficulty," said Philip soberly. "He is not tall,—small for his age, I should say, but likely to start up some day and grow like a weed; and he will be pale enough to please you when he gets up from his illness. As to the gew-gaws, they might easily be hired at any theatrical outfitter's, and Jim's curls would grow longer if your mother wouldn't cut them off. There are some radical differences, I admit, between your favourite and Jimmie, but Jim's the better fellow."

"You don't say so!" exclaimed the amazed Jane Maria.

"I do, emphatically. Don't you see, Miss Jennie that your Lord Fitz Walter is a milk-sop, while Jim is a little man?"

It was evident that Jane failed to appreciate the distinction. Philip looked half quizzically, half pityingly at the lank, awkward girl who stood in the dimly-lighted, homely kitchen, leaning her arms on the high back of an old-fashioned chair. The tall clock in the corner ticked monotonously, and she remained motionless, lost in her silly dreams.

"Poor child! Poor overworked drudge! No wonder she clings to her Fitz Walters and spangles and aristocratic pallor, as a contrast to her daily life," thought Philip. "Yet this half-awakened affection for Jim might be utilized, perhaps."

"Yes," he continued, "Jim is a pretty good boy as boys go. I like him. Miss Doane likes him. He is likely to have a hard time of it too. Miss Jennie, he has been the plague of your life, and will be again, no doubt. His angelic wings have not yet sprouted. But you can be of use to him if you want to be; and if you watch Miss Doane, who has had more experience as a nurse than you, you will soon see just what to do."

"Yes, sir. She's handy and spry, ain't she? I can't be like her."

" No two people are alike ; but you are Jim's
sister, and it is the thing, I suppose, for sisters to
take care of brothers when they are ill. If you
do not know how, you can learn ; only do not bury
yourself in the 'Haunted Homes of Hillsdale.' I'll
tell you what. If you will let that trash alone, I
will send you a box of books when I get back
to the city, enough to last you all winter. But do
not go about dreaming of your magnificent, high-
flown friends, or you will spill Jim's medicine and
burn his gruel. There is not room enough in the
cottage, just now, for your family, Miss Doane, and
me, and Lord What's-his-name, my Lady Terra-
pin, and Fitz Milk-sop. Let's crowd the nobility
out, Miss Jennie."

He spoke in a good-humoured, jesting way, as he
had sometimes before done with regard to these
same lofty personages.

" I know I'm always a-forgettin' after I've been
a-readin'. I won't read another word while Jim's
sick," she said earnestly.

" That is a good, sensible girl. Good-night." And,
taking his candle, Philip went to his room with a
consciousness that he was rapidly learning to adapt
himself to curious and unforeseen circumstances,
and not knowing which was the oddest position for
a hitherto solitary and self-absorbed young bachelor
to fill,—that of keeper of the terrific harpy,
errand-boy and slave of his brilliant young enemy,
or assuager of the tears of rustic maidenhood.

He heard nothing as he passed Gem's room ; but
later, from time to time, various sounds reached
him, Leigh's light, rapid step as she ministered

to the wants of the invalid, her voice with its low, caressing cadence, an occasional weary word from Gem. Through the long night-watches her patient care was unremitting. She had opened the door that Gem might have more air; and far into the morning, softly, yet distinctly through the quiet house came the words of a song she was singing.

> "Clear and cool, clear and cool,
> By laughing shallow and dreaming pool.
> Cool and clear, cool and clear,
> By shining shingle and foaming weir,"

rippled the tender voice, and the restless child lay hushed and calmed.

> "Undefiled for the undefiled;
> Play by me, bathe in me, mother and child."

And the pure, sweet tones "echoed along the vacant hall," and found a resting-place above in the heart of the silent listener.

Pained and sad, like the burden of her song, was the girl's voice as she sang the second verse; and

> "Who dare sport with the sin-defiled?
> Shriuk from me, turn from me, mother and child!"

came almost with a shudder.

> "Strong and free, strong and free,
> The floodgates are open away to the sea,
> Free and strong, free and strong,
> Cleansing my streams as I hurry along
> To the golden sands and the leaipng bar
> And the taintless tide that awaits me afar."

Clearer and fuller rang the voice in the glad rush of the song, and

> "As I lose myself in the infinite main,
> Like a soul that has sinned and is pardoned again."

sounded so full of a passionate joy, that Philip asked himself, wonderingly—

"What does that white-souled child, voiced like heaven's lark, know of sin, that she sings with such a depth of feeling about the joy of a pardoned soul?"

> "Undefiled for the undefiled,
> Play by me, bathe in me, mother and child."

floated up in the tender, restful tone again, and then the voice died away. All was quiet. Gem was asleep. The cocks were crowing, and the first faint tokens of the dawn showing in the east, before Philip closed his eyes. And, though touched by the melody which rose so sweetly through the stillness of the night, yet he hardened his heart and resolved to hearken as often as possible to the voice of the charmer, but not to be a whit deceived, charmed she never so wisely. Fair and gracious and womanly was the outward effect of keeping her loving vigils by the side of the suffering child. But might it not be a dissolving view? Was it pure goodness, or only another caprice?

CHAPTER XIII.

"The exquisite,
Brown, blessed eyes."
—JEAN INGELOW.

EDGECOMB, Sunday, August 12, 18—.

DEAR TOM,—Some men achieve meanness, and some have meanness thrust upon them. To the latter class I belong, being forced to tell tales of your sister, or, by remaining silent, to virtually approve of the bad state of things down here. Miss Doane, no doubt, frankly gives her view of the matter ; but people see things differently. She is hovering over the bedside of our common friend Jim. You know, of course, who Jim is, and Miss Doane's regard for Jim, and Jim's varied fascinations ; but, granting that he is Phœbus Apollo himself, it does not follow that Miss Doane should throw herself under his chariot wheels and be crushed in pieces. If she would content herself with flitting in and out of the room in an atmosphere of airy beneficence, smiles, and flowers, after the approved fashion of young women upon the stage, I should not trouble myself to report at headquarters. The facts are these : She stays day and night. She has a steady, business-like air which fills me with amazement. She evinces a determination to remain until the last gun is fired, and, worst of all, she *works*. My humble remonstrance, once offered, had no more effect upon her than the idle wind, and I have not the honour of being sufficiently in Miss Doane's good graces to take the liberty of expressing my opinion a second time. Never, apparently, was there a young woman more benevolent, more efficient, more exclusively governed by her own ideas and wishes, and more directly on the road to tiring herself out and getting ill.

All of which is respectfully submitted.

Yours,
PHILIP.

Miles and miles from Edgecomb, in a pretty breakfast room, where everything was charming except the temperature, this letter was read by the persons whom Miss Doane's conduct most nearly affected.

Tom read it. Bessie read it. They looked at each other inquiringly.

" Well, Tom ? "

" Madam, it is not well ; it is ill. It is reprehensible ; it is pernicious. Next week, the majesty of the law—which is I—and the claim of family affection—which is you—will fall like a thunderbolt upon the misguided girl."

" Like two thunderbolts, Tom, dear. But don't get eloquent. It's too warm, and it makes your forehead shine. Please don't mistake me for an enlightened jury. I'm sure I don't see why you should. I don't look like one. Eat another peach, and calm yourself, my liege."

" Your *which ?* Did I understand you to say your liege ? Heavens and earth ! What fiendish sarcasm is this ? "

" Did I not tell you, dear, that it makes your forehead shine unbecomingly to exert yourself so much ? "

" Madam, that moisture which offends your weakly fastidious eye emanates from and betrays the workings of my massive intellect, which is now trying to solve this problem : Why did I marry a woman who had such a sister ? "

" You married me, my beloved, because you could not help yourself,—I was so perfectly bewitching. And I married you because I was not so well acquainted as I now am with the glaring defects in your character. As for Leigh, she is doing exactly right, as she always does, and you know it."

" I know, and evidently Ogden knows, that she is a perverse and headstrong girl, and you are as illogical as the rest of your charming sex—whose abject slave, I will remark in parenthesis, I am— in deserting the man you promised to honour and obey, and enrolling under Leigh's banner when you do not know the circumstances."

" Oh! Oh! Oh! " exclaimed Bessie, despairingly. " Did ever a man, since the earth was made, talk ten minutes without dragging in what he calls our want of logic ? And what does logic amount to, I'd like to know ? And who cares about logic ? It is not logic that we are discussing,—it is Leigh, and she is doing perfectly right."

" My love, allow me to suggest that you take another peach and calm yourself. Your manner lacks tranquillity. The ladies of the Vere de Vere family were never known to talk the crimp out of their hair, as my friend Mr. Tennyson feelingly remarks. Believe me, my fair one, your former elegant indolence was more becoming."

" Tom, you are a provoking boy. Now, why is it not quite as logical in me to side with Leigh, without positively knowing all the circumstances, as it is for you to agree with Mr. Ogden simply because he's a man."

"But I thought logic was barred out of this conversation."

"Dear, if you can possibly control that giant intellect for which you, and you only, entertain such profound reverence, stop its 'rare and radiant' witticisms for ten minutes and listen to me. Of course Leigh is right, and she will not be ill, for she never was."

"Magnificent reasoning. Incontrovertible," muttered Tom. "She never died, but I presume—"

"Be quiet, you wretched boy. I'm talking now. Leigh is perfectly right, and—"

"My dear, dear Bessie, nothing in the world affords me such pure delight as the sound of your beloved voice; but you have said and reiterated 'Leigh is right,' so many times, that I must remind you that 'the dignity of truth is lost in much protesting.'"

"When you are afraid of being routed utterly, you always quote Shakespeare at me. He is your last resort; but I know, the moment you begin to brandish him, it is a confession of weakness on your part, and he doesn't intimidate me in the least. Now, sir, I will inform you—as I should have done, some time ago, if you had not interfered and interrupted and enjoyed hearing yourself talk—that we will start for Edgecomb Monday morning; and what I have been trying to tell you is that I had determined to go then, anyway, before Mr. Ogden's letter came."

"You had, had you ? You bold and resolute woman ! You Semiramis—you Judith—you Artemisia—"

" I believe those are all the names you know, dear, without referring to the 'Famous Women of Antiquity.' You'll find it at the right of the fourth shelf in the library," suggested Bessie, with a most impudent drawl.

" ' Entreat me not to leave thee,' " sang Tom, mockingly.

"Certainly not, if you'll be sensible. Really, Tom, I am not afraid Leigh will be ill, though I shall do all I can to relieve her. I am so glad to go away from this hot, dusty city. We must go, if we are ever going. And, Tom dear, I'm so happy that you can go too."

" Perfidious woman, no blandishments ! You were actually intending to go without me."

" Certainly."

" And you mean to help Leigh in her nefarious undertaking ? "

"That is my intention."

" And she is absolute perfection, as usual ? "

" She is."

" And Ogden and I are imbeciles ? "

" If you fancy the word,—yes."

" My dear, I will drag my crushed atoms into the library, and answer Ogden's letter."

He withdrew, only to return in a moment, and put his head in the door for a parting shot.

" Mrs. Otis, I have just discovered the grand mistake of my life. Instead of marrying you, and having you and your sister agree in thought, word, and deed, *ad nauseam*, and thereby make my life miserable, I ought to have married both of you, and emigrated to Utah, and then you would fight deliciously, and I should have some peace. 'Happy thought!' It may not be too late!"

"You goose! Leigh wouldn't look at you!"

Mr. Otis bowed his vanquished head, departed, wrote to his friend as follows :—

WEDNESDAY, August 15, 18—.

MY DEAR OGDEN,—Yours received. Heaven only knows what the women will do next. My wife says she is going to Edgecomb next week, to be a ministering spirit like unto her sister, and I expect the two together will twang their angelic harp-strings in our ears, and vex our righteous souls. Can't anything be done to hurry the youngster into a comfortable convalescence? Blake's yacht will be around there in the course of a couple of weeks, and the girls are good sailors, and would like a trip more than anything, if they could be torn from their crotchets and that boy. I flatter myself I have some influence upon each individually. Together, they are stronger than the rock of Gibraltar, and I the most helpless and victimized of men. I rely on you to poison young Holbrook, or get him well instanter. We shall probably arrive Wednesday next.

Yours,

TOM.

And Bessie wrote :—

LEIGH, DEAR,—We shall actually leave Monday, and Tom is making the same charming announcement to your Mr. Ogden, who, by the way, says that you are working too hard, and that you will be ill, and that you have a will of your own—and what would you be worth

J

if you had not, I'd like to inquire ! Tom and I have just had a delicious little tiff about you, and I wouldn't have you ill *now* for anything in the world, because those two superior beings have declared you will be. You won't, will you, dear ? Is the poor boy having a very hard time ? I have missed your long letters so, lately, and the sea-breezes they seemed to bring with them. Never again will I be a dutiful wife, and wait for Tom—never ! But it would have been hard for the dear old boy to stay here without me to torment him, wouldn't it ? He would have been so lonely I'm glad I waited, and perhaps we'll enjoy everything all the more, after the delay and the doubt. I am perfectly wild to see you, and so curious about Edgecomb, and the farm-house where Gem is, and the long girl, and the dreadful woman, and especially about Mr. Ogden. You do not rave about him so violently as you did, but it must be extremely annoying to meet him constantly after all that has happened. It's too bad, dear ! And if he's on the yacht, it will ruin the trip for you, will it not ? If only Tom and Mr. Blake did not think so much of him ; but they depend upon his going. If he had the slightest delicacy he would not join the party. But that, of course, is too much to expect of such a person. However, I will not let any gloomy foreboding interfere with my present delight. Sufficient unto the day is the Ogden thereof. It will be happiness enough to see you and breathe some pure air, and the Idlewild may sink in the "vasty deep" before it reaches Edgecomb. Who knows ? And there isn't time to write or hear from you again. Blessed thought ! We shall see you, I believe, Wednesday, and no one in the world will be so happy as

Your loving

BESSIE.

Philip found this letter, with Tom's, one rainy evening, when he took his accustomed tramp to the

post-office, and upon his return he sent it in to
Leigh, who received it with delight, read it smilingly, but afterwards sat silent and thoughtful,
with the open letter in her hand, while Jane, who
had learned, under the young lady's kind and careful guidance, to do many helpful things tolerably
well, arranged Gem's pillow and gave him his medicine and drink. Again Leigh read, "It must be
extremely annoying to meet him constantly," and,
" If he is on the yacht it will ruin the trip for you."
These statements were clear and strong, and author-
ized by herself, for Bessie's views were necessarily
but reflections of her own. Was it so, then?
Would she be sorry to have him on the yacht?
For ten days, now, she had been with Gem. During that time, she had done what she could for the
boy, too busy to pause and analyze the condition
of things, striving only to avoid the Holbrook
quicksands. She had thought little of herself, less
perhaps of Philip, yet unconsciously had depended
much upon him. It was natural. He was the only
person of her caste within reach. Yet Bessie's letter
surprised her. She did not think Mr. Ogden obtuse and intrusive. Her old self and her new self
had met, and were staring at each other unpleasantly. She must tell Bessie what Mr. Ogden had
done for her, and Bessie must be grateful to him as
she was. Bessie must know how thoughtful he had
been, and that he had saved her from so very many
annoyances, and that he had quietly ruled the
whole queer household, and that if ever she found
it necessary to ask him to do anything for her, he
did what she wished as if they had always known

each other, and it was the most natural thing in
the world that he should do it. She had grown
accustomed to the grave, steady look he wore when
there was any real need of him in the sick-room, as
well as to the appreciative, quick glance with which
he would respond to the involuntary appeal for
sympathy which her eyes would make when prominent traits in the Holbrook family were too
ludicrously shown. Leigh was in a strange mood.
She did not understand herself. But it would be
only fair to tell Bessie that Mr. Ogden's absence
would not increase her enjoyment on the yacht.
A knock interrupted her revery. Jane Maria opened the door.

"May I come in ?" said Philip, pausing on the
threshold and looking in pleased surprise upon the
pretty scene. A bright fire of hemlock bark burned on the hearth, and threw flickering lights and
shadows over the room, giving an ideal grace to
the rough walls and stiff furniture. Gem's face,
looking at him from the pillows, as he approached
the bed, was thin and pale, with large eager eyes,
and the hand which the child held out to him was
that of a pathetic and spiritualized Jim, such as he
had never expected to see.

"And how's the boy to-night ?"

"Pretty smart. She's a-sayin' things and a-sing-
in'. You'd ought ter hear her. You stay, an'
she'll keep on ?" said Gem, languidly.

Philip turned, and looked inquiringly at Leigh.

"Certainly you may stay, Mr. Ogden, if you like.
You need never wait for my invitation. Gem is
host."

" I would like to stay if I will not be in the way. How cheerful you are in here ! It is rather a bad night out. That fire is an inspiration. Yours, I presume, Miss Doane ? "

" Yes ; it was so gloomy and cold, and the damp breezes would creep in everywhere, and I thought a fire might please Gem, and, to be honest, I wanted it myself too. Jane kindly brought in the bark, and I made it. Isn't it pretty ? Gem thinks it's great fun. He seems really better, does he not ? "

Philip replied in a low bow. " He does seem bright just now, but he is very variable, you know. The doctor said—"

" Ah ! don't, please," she interrupted with a little imploring gesture. " Do prophesy smooth things to-night. Gem is better. He is really, and that makes me happy ; and they are coming next week, Mr. Ogden,—my sister and my brother,— and that makes me almost too happy. And it *is* pleasant here to-night, is it not ? Hear the wind tearing about outside and the rain coming down in torrents. I like to listen to the storm, because my Gem is so comfortable, and my fire is so lovely."

She spoke rapidly. Her cheeks were flushed, and her eyes bright with excitement.

" You do look very happy," Philip said kindly, " and you have been a little pale and weary for a day or two, have you not ? "

Leigh, suddenly grave, looked with downcast eyes into the flames.

" Have you not been tired, lately, Miss Doane ? " he continued. " You never admit that you are fatigued, but your face has told tales of you."

" So have you, it seems, Mr. Ogden." And she
looked up quickly with a smile.

" Ah ! my sin has found me out ! But you pardon me because of the happy result ? "

" I will pardon you next Wednesday, when the
happy result will be an accomplished fact. I shall
be happy enough to forgive anybody for anything."

" It will be a good day, then, for malefactors to
present themselves before you ? " And a vein of
earnestness ran through the light words.

" Happiness ought to make one good, Mr. Ogden.
I am not good ; but perhaps my blessings, Wednesday, will render me not only willing to forgive,
but—to be forgiven—which is harder—sometimes."
Then, as if she had said more than she meant, feeling
rather than seeing Philip's intent look, she turned
away hastily, and taking some great pieces of bark
from a basket by the chimney, threw them one by
one upon the blazing fire.

" Don't you like to hear it crackle ? " she gayly
asked.

" I like everything, to-night," said Philip, with
more warmth in his voice than Leigh had ever
heard. She said nothing, but heaped more bark,
piece by piece, upon the blaze ; and Philip admiringly watched her pretty movements, and the delighted child-smile upon her face. The brilliant
light illumined the whole room. Jane was occupied with Gem ; the rain fell heavily outside.
Where Leigh and Philip stood there was silence ;
and for one brief moment, to both, the storm without, and Gem and his sister, seemed far away, and
they two standing together in the firelight were

nearer than ever before. But the moment passed, and, with it, its glow and warmth and pleasant sense of nearness.

"Miss Leigh," said a faint little voice, 'wasn't that a jolly one ? Jest as good as a bonfire."

"O Gem dear, didn't it hurt your eyes ? I was very thoughtless."

"Well, it hurt 'em a little, p'r'aps; but I wish you'd blaze her up again. It's fun."

"I must not, dear ; shut the poor eyes, do. You shall have ever so much more fun than this as soon as you are strong again," she said, as a consolation.

"Indeed, you shall, Jim," said Philip, heartily.

"Yes, Jimmie, you shall," chimed in Jane Maria, by way of further encouragement.

"O, come now," said Gem, with a touch of the old sauciness, "just let a feller alone, won't yer ! I ain't a baby; if I am sick, and I ain't a goin' to cry cos Miss Leigh won't blaze up that ere bark. Miss Leigh, I'll shut my eyes as tight as a drum if you'll sing some more."

And Leigh sang the songs the boy liked best, without, apparently, a thought of Philip, who drew his chair back from the hearth and sat in the shade, while the firelight played fitfully about her, now falling upon the dainty hands, clasped lightly in her lap, now aspiring, gleaming about the white throat, and revealing, for a moment, the fair hair and dark earnest eyes, then sinking humbly to her feet. She did not sing transcendental, mystical love-songs. She had found that they were too fearful and wonderful for Gem,—as indeed they are for many of us,—and that they did not affect him pleasantly. He was, if uneducated, an honest critic, who unhesitatingly expressed his mind. A contented, quiet smile would indicate his approval, while a contemptuous " Pooh, ain't no sense in it !" would suggest to Leigh the efficacy of changing her theme. She admired his frank, boyish scorn of things he did not understand or like, and she exerted herself to please him far more than she was accustomed to try to please some of her drawing-room critics, who received her best or poorest musical efforts with the invariable "How charming !" and without a ray of real enthusiasm. She had learned to know Gem's favourites well. Songs with pictures and stories in them pleased him; songs that did not almost end, and then wander along helplessly and aimlessly and die away by degrees, but that stopped short when they were done ; and especially songs with a "jingle." Leigh had gone far back into past years, and brought out, for Gem's pleasure, scraps of melody she had not sung since her childhood. A motley throng of subjects her voice conjured up as she sat singing before the fire; in a queer chair a hundred years old, whose straight, narrow back, surmounted by white wooden knobs with brass tops, rose far above her head. She sang bird-songs and boat-songs, cradle-songs and echo-songs, ballads about girls at spinning-wheels, and knights and shepherdesses and some swinging old cavalier tunes that suggested the clatter of horses' hoofs, and once—Philip in his dark corner smiled to hear the bubbling, sparkling thing under a new England roof—a bit of a French drinking-song, which Gem liked for its gay, ringing melody, and which Leigh did not translate.

After a while Gem, soothed by the familiar tones, fell asleep. Jane stole quietly from the room. Leigh sang gradually lower and lower, that a sudden silence might not rouse the child. She turned, listened a moment to his breathing, then leaned her head back with a long sigh. Philip came softly forward.

" You are very tired, Miss Doane."

" O, no ! " said Leigh, without glancing up.

" But that deep-drawn sigh ? "

" There was no rhyme nor reason in it," she said, a little drearily.

Philip stood looking doubtfully at her.

" You do not believe me, do you, Mr. Ogden ? "

" If I do not, you would not think me very civil to say so. It would be a base return for your kindness in allowing me to hear you sing."

" But I was not singing to you,"—looking up for the first time with her little audacious air. " I sang to my Gem. Those were his own particular songs. Anybody who cared, might listen, of course. But I might make a different selection for you."

" Pardon me. I knew very well you did not sing to me. But the ' anybody ' who cared to listen was as grateful as if you had specially dedicated every song to him, and if you would make a different selection for me you would make a mistake. They were Gem's songs, but they were mine too. I claim them, and I shall keep them. I have the most profound respect for your will, Miss Doane. It is a mighty power. But there are some things which even you cannot accomplish. You cannot recall the pleasure those songs have given me, nor can you convince me that you are not a very weary, over-worked young lady."

Leigh was not in a mood to question his right to say this, and it was impossible for her not to feel the kindness in his voice. She did not stop to ask herself why she should or should not open her heart to him as she rose impulsively and said :

" I am not tired, Mr. Ogden. At least I do not think I am. I am perfectly well and strong, only I am not sure but that I'm—homesick. It's very absurd, I know, and weak. I am quite ashamed of myself," she went on, with a little quiver in her voice.

Philip said nothing, simply because he knew not what to say. They stood in silence, while the queer shadows danced about the room. Leigh continued, without the faintest consciousness that she was doing anything unusual, and, meeting the young man's gaze quite frankly,—

" I forgot it when Bessie's letter came. I was more than happy ; but now it has come back, the dreary feeling. I never was away from her in my life before, you know—and I feel very, very far away ; and it has been so long, and I know I am perfectly ridiculous, but I do not think I can help it." And, much to her own surprise, two great tears crept into her eyes, and still she stood smiling frankly at Philip.

" Poor child ! " he said involuntarily ; then turned away and paced up and down the room. He saw it all now ; of course it had been hard for her. Not a soul for whom she cared, except Gem, in the place. Young, inexperienced, and, in spite of her self-reliant ways, dependent upon her home-life. Days and days, perhaps, she had been forlorn and desolate at heart, while her face had worn the pretty little cool smile, as she gracefully parried occasional unpleasant thrusts from Mrs. Holbrook, patiently trained the willing but inefficient Jane in the way she should go, and "compassed" Gem with "sweet observances." It had not once occurred to him but that she was enjoying her strange experience, after a fashion. She was a brave girl, and only a girl, after all, as she stood in a dejected, drooping way, looking sadly down upon the brass andirons as if she could read a gloomy prophecy in their shining tops. If she were not so physically weary that she had unconsciously reached out for sympathy, he knew that she would not have confided in him. How dull he had been, and hard, actually arming himself against the fresh young thing! Had she not had a right to dislike him, and to manifest her dislike plainly, if she wished? He walked to the bed and looked at Gem, to the window and stared out into the night, then returning to Leigh stood waiting for her to speak. Suddenly she began with a pretty petulance—

"Isn't it just like a woman to go and do the thing she wishes to do, and do it the very way she wished to do it, and then cry about it and complain?" And she looked as bright as a May morning. Philip smiled.

"But you have not cried, Miss Doane."

"Not quite," she said; and again her eyes filled with tears; "but, as you see, I am ineffably silly."

"Miss Doane," said Philip, really concerned, "this has all been too much for you—too great a strain. Pardon me, but you seemed so cool, so perfectly self-reliant, it never occurred to me that you could be losing your courage."

"But I've not lost it," she returned with some spirit. "I do not know what is the matter with me to-night. I was tolerably good when I felt so strangely here at first, and things were hard, and I was anxious about Gem, and did not know when my sister would come ; and now, when there is not the slightest reason, I break down in this absurd way."

"Poor child !" said Philip again. And Leigh forgot to resent the words or the tone. Then he said lightly : "Unfortunately, we cannot always control our moods, Miss Doane. No doubt, your fit of the blues is inopportune, as you say. So was Jim's illness, according to our friend, Mrs. Holbrook. We are creatures of circumstance, knocked about in spite of ourselves."

"But you must think me very foolish."

"You must think me very dull not to have seen this before."

"You ? Why should you, and what difference would it have made ?"

"Not much, I presume ; but I might have been able to make things easier, and to be of some use."

"O, Mr. Ogden, you have been very good ! Do you not know that you have ?" said Leigh, warmly. "I have not said much about it, but I am not ungrateful. Indeed I am not."

"Have I really been good to you ?" he asked,

with perhaps more eagerness than was quite necessary "for Gem's sake." Leigh blushed and, with
a slight effort, said,—

"Only Gem and I know how good." He saw
she used Gem's name as a shield. Again he thoughtfully paced the room.

"Miss Doane, I have done nothing for you or for
Gem which deserves any remembrance. You over-
estimate trifling services that cost me nothing. Yet
I would presume to ask a favour on the strength of
them, for I fear it is my only hope of influencing
you. Am I ungenerous to wish to be paid?"

"Very," said Leigh, mischievously.

"But not unreasonable?"

"Possibly not. It depends upon what you are
going to ask." Then, with the sudden softening of
manner which Philip was beginning to find bewitching and dangerous, "I think I shall say yes.
You are really kind. I do not deserve that you
should be so kind," she added slowly. Again, in
the careless, smiling way: "But we do not get
exactly what we deserve, any of us,—do we? It is
always either more or less. I hope I shall never
have my just dues,—for I should get such a wee
grain from the sugar-plums of life. It is not grand
to say so, but I do not want to see the beauty of
renunciation. I want to see the sugar-plums."

Philip listened, glad to hear the merry tone
again; but he noted that after she spoke the smile
died quickly from her face.

"You are plainly tired out," he said, earnestly.
"Do not think me presuming, but I must interfere. I should insist upon driving you to Miss

Phipps's, late as it is, if there were not a storm. You think I would not succeed ?" he added, as Leigh looked incredulous. "But you do not know what a tyrant I am when I am roused, and I am thoroughly roused to-night, I assure you."

"Do you scratch and bite, or only growl, Mr. Ogden ?"

"I carry my point amiably, if I can; if not—" He shook his head menacingly, as a substitute for words.

"Curious preface to asking a favour," said Leigh.

"Ah ! it was to be a favour, was it not ? As a favour, then, may I speak to Miss Jennie, and let her make some arrangement for you to-night. That den in there "—pointing to a little room which opened out of Gem's and where Leigh occasionally snatched an hour's sleep—"is no place for you to-night."

"Gem will not be much care ; see how well he sleeps."

"I am going to stay here myself to-night," Philip said decidedly.

"Such a pretty, gracious way of asking a favour ! So deprecating and humble !" she retorted.

"I beg your pardon," said Philip, laughing. "I do not intend to be brusque, but I am very much in earnest. I shall stay, and you must go. A good night's rest is what you need and what you must have."

"Don't say another word. You apologize, and then offend more deeply every moment. Three 'musts' in a row ! No one ever says 'must' to me. Do you really drive me away ?"

" Certainly not. At least, not yet. I am asking you to go as a favour, at present, you know."

" Go I must, evidently," laughed Leigh ; " and I think it will be more graceful, as well as the part of wisdom, to grant the favour rather than be ignominiously expelled. I shall take pleasure, Mr. Ogden, in obliging you and speaking to Jane myself." Philip bowed his thanks, and said,—

" Will you add to my indebtedness by going at once ? "

" I would vanish up the chimney if I knew how ; but being only a mortal maiden, you must give me time to collect some of my belongings," Leigh answered, passing into the other room. Returning, she looked long and earnestly at Gem, and arranged a few articles on a little table at his side, then stood still. " You understand about the medicine, Mr. Ogden."

" I think I understand everything I am expected to, except why — "

" Why I do not go ? "

" Exactly, if I may be so bold."

" Because we are creatures of habit, and it is my habit to stay here ; and because I am used to my own way, and it is not my way to leave Gem."

Philip declined further argument. With mock ceremony he opened the door, and stood with the air of one waiting to bow her out of the room.

" I am not at all sure that you are even a very polite tyrant," said Leigh ; " but I am really going now. Good night, Mr. Ogden. Perhaps I *am* a little tired," she added. Philip smiled, and held out his hand.

"Good-night, Miss Doane, and pleasant dreams, and thank you for everything," he said earnestly, as her hand rested in his a moment.

Philip closed the door after her, heaped more bark on the fire, and sat down. From the flame, from the ashes, from the dark corners of the room, everywhere he saw looking out at him a pair of great, honest, brown eyes, smiling through their tears. He knew her now for what she was, he told himself. He had wasted all these precious days in misconceiving her, in arrogantly presuming to judge her. He would never be mistaken again. She might be merry or sad, "or that sweet calm that is just between." She might assume, at will, her bright or sombre chameleon colours, might one moment be stately as a queen, the next humble as a little child, yet through all changes he would know her. In her sweet, earnest eyes, he had seen a blessed vision of her true heart. What was he, that she should care for him ; yet, could he teach those eyes to look kindly at him on his own hearthstone, he would ask nothing more of Fate.

CHAPTER XIV.

"There's a pang in all rejoicing,
A joy in the heart of pain."

" TOM, isn't it delightful? Nurse, don't attempt to get down with baby in your arms. Mr. Otis will take him. Why where is Leigh?" And talking rapidly every moment, Mrs. Otis put her pretty head out of the stage window, and eagerly scrutinized Miss Phipps's abode.

The driver swung open the door. The Otis family, an interesting group, and the Otis paraphernalia, an imposing pile of trunks, baskets, bags, and wraps, were deposited at the gate.

"Why, Tom, where is she? Where can she be?" asked Bessie, in keen disappointment, regarding her husband with an air of suspicion, as if he had spirited Leigh away.

"And where's the Phipps, which is more to the purpose? She's the one about whom I feel most concerned. No Phipps, no dinner?" said Tom, ruefully, stalking through the deserted house with the wondering Bessie behind him. "Careless tenants they! Let's take the silver and go. I'll plead emotional insanity, induced by jolting fifteen miles in that diabolical stage-coach, a hot August day."

"Tom, dear! don't joke any more. It's that little boy," said Bessie, gravely. "He must be

K

worse. Nothing else in the world would keep
Leigh."

"My dear, I'm strongly inclined to think that I
might continue to joke, even if that little boy
should die, because I never saw him, you know,
and I haven't enough over-soul to feel very miserable about the little chap. But I imagine you are
right. What are you going to do about it?"

"We'll go up stairs, and get the least bit settled,
and I'll see that nurse and baby are comfortable,
and while you attend to the trunks I'll find something for you to eat." Tom smiled admiringly.

"Bessie, for a woman who crimps her hair and
looks awfully superficial, you do occasionaly evince
an uncommon amount of practical wisdom. Upon
my word, I never heard anything neater in my
life than that last hint of yours."

"And afterwards," continued Bessie, "you must
take me to Leigh. Help me up stairs, dear. I'm
tired. And then have the trunks brought up, if
the driver has come back." As they passed the door,
she said, "Will you look at him? Actually, he's
reposing, complacently, on my 'Saratoga,' with my
gray shawl for a pillow, and waiting for you to help
him, is he not? He has brought no one with him."

"Yes I presume he expects me to reward him
liberally for allowing me the privilege of shoulder
ing my own baggage. I always thought I should
like Arcadia," continued Tom, sentimentally. "These
ingenuous ways appeal to my better nature. I
wish I had a shepherd's crook with a blue ribbon
on it. I would like to artlessly punch the head of
that recumbent youth."

They began to ascend the stairs. On the old-fashioned landing, from which arose two smaller flights, branching off to the right and left, Tom stopped short with a terrific shudder.

"Can't do it, Bessie. Can't go a step farther. I'm afraid, mortally afraid. There's a silence—a spell—a what do you call it—in this fateful mansion. Don't you feel a grewsome chill penetrating your marrow?"

"I feel dusty and travel-stained, and as if I should like to change my dress. Send that man up with the small hat-box and my travelling-bag, will you, dear?"

"But, you prosaic, sordid, petty soul, where, O where do you imagine all these doors lead? What hateful Errinys broods over our wanderings? What mysteries are hidden behind these heavy oaken panels, what thrilling tales of blood and doom, what thing-um-bobs!" he ejaculated in a stage whisper.

"If you must indulge in flights of fancy at this inopportune time, the correct thing would be to liken the house to an enchanted palace. I have a suspicion your language is borrowed from a dime-novel."

"No, my love, from Thoth," remarked Tom, solemnly.

"And who, or what, in the world is Thoth?"

"Thoth, my poor ignorant spouse," explained Tom, with a bewildering and triumphant smile, "was the god of eloquence of the ancient Egyptians, from which elegant and exclusive race, by the way, the Otis family is descended. We have our gene-

alogy complete, an unbroken line, preserved, on
papyrus, from an epoch anterior to the reign of the
Hyksos. Thoth is a considerably older and more
aristocratic deity than Apollo. You didn't know
it, did you, poor dear?"

" I never could account for it before," said Bessie,
coolly ignoring his tone of commiseration, and
gravely scrutinizing her husband's genial countenance, " but now I know why, sometimes, your
features in repose remind me of an Egyptian mum-
my; but you cannot help it, can you, poor dear?
Tom, we are dreadfully silly. Do hurry with that
hat-box, or I shall go down myself." Tom descended
three stairs obediently, and halted. Bessie had
glanced into Leigh's room, recognised it, then had
entered her own and thrown herself, gratefully,
into the open arms of the big chair, the only thing
in the house that seemed to expect and welcome
her.

" Bessie," called Tom from the stairs, " before I
go a step farther, I want to know one thing. You,
with your usual felicity of expression, liken this
house to an enchanted palace. May I, O, may I
imprint a tender kiss upon the lips of the sleeping
beauty, if I find one, as I undoubtedly shall in this
mysterious place? Have I your full and free permission, to be followed by no tearful, jealous re-
proaches?"

" Certainly, my gallant young prince, certainly,"
said Bessie, graciously. " You'll find the fairest
of the fair asleep in nurse's arms, down stairs; but
don't wake him, please. And Tom," she added,
choking with laughter, " there's another one—

don't have any scruples on my account—that man
sound asleep out on my trunks. You may wake
him as soon as you please."

" Bother !" said Tom.

" Dear, was that classic quotation prevalent
among the ancient Egyptians, and suggested by
your friend Thoth?" came languidly from the depths
of the great chair, in the sweetest voice imaginable.
" Poor boy ! You seem to need to invoke his aid
often enough, even now. What will you do when
Leigh comes ? "

" I am going to interest myself, at once, in Cory-
don and the trunks," was the meek response. "'Some
griefs gnaw deep,' and for ' some woes ' work is the
only means of relief."

An hour after, they were driving to the Holbrook cottage. It was about six, the close of a
hotter day than often came to breezy Edgecomb,
even in August. Upon the road they met some of
the village folk, and were greeted with supernaturally solemn stares.

" I believe Leigh is right," said Tom. " There is
something uncanny about this place. I don't blame
her for being belligerent in this atmosphere, Moses
himself would feel pugnacious here."

" It is the dust in your throat that makes you
cross, dear," suggested the practical Bessie. " Everything does seem new and strange, but I fancy it is
only because there was no one to meet us at the
house. That child must be very ill."

" I should say so," ejaculated Tom. " Behold the
vultures ? " indicating several groups of people

standing silently, or talking in low and ominous
tones, at a little distance from the cottage.

"Hush, dear, they mean it kindly."

"But what are we going to do now ?" asked Tom,
dubiously, as they stood by the roadside near where
he had fastened his horse.   "We certainly have no
intention of going in where Leigh is, and perhaps
she cannot come out.   Hadn't we better go back ?
We can do no good here," he said, with a man's
impatience at the anomalous position.

"We will wait a moment," answered Bessie,
quietly.   "I think Leigh will come., Perhaps she
will see us.   Dear, look ; little Gem must be there
where the windows are so wide open and the people
are moving about,—and oh ! Tom, dear, what is
that ? Isn't it he groaning ?"   And she sank down
on the bank, putting her hands over her ears.
"How can these people have the heart to stay so
near, only to listen to such dreadful sounds !"

"The Evil One himself brought us here, but in
spite of him and his works you are going back,"
muttered Tom, turning the horse. "Pretty ending
to the hard day you've had. I don't mean that the
ghouls and vampires shall gloat over you, my dear ;
and they will if you stay here much longer."

A tall, angular person left her place among the
women who stood nearest the house, and, approaching a window, beckoned to some one within.

"Come, Bessie," said Tom.

"Wait one moment, dear. If Leigh does not
come, I will go." But Leigh came. In answer
to the summons she appeared at the door. Under
the thick hop-vines that climbed over the porch she
stood one instant, pale, erect, with widely open

eyes. She did not need the gesture from Miss Phipps that indicated where she should look for her sister. She passed the waiting, watching neighbours as if she saw them not, and, with closely-set lips and a hard, strained look in her eyes, went rapidly through the gate and down the road, and flung herself into her sister's arms without one word of greeting.

"I must go back now," she said.

"Ah, dear, not so soon," pleaded Bessie; "you look so ill." She dared not ask how Gem was. His pitiful moans reached them through the stillness. Bessie shuddered, but Leigh's face looked gray and hard, as if carven out of granite.

"It is dreadful to hear him, is it not?" she said; "but he does not know. The doctor says he is not conscious of his suffering."

"Is there no hope?" asked Tom.

"Very little," said Leigh, in a dry, mechanical tone. "He has been this way for days. He will do that hours longer; but we shall know before morning."

"Ah! there's Ogden," exclaimed Tom. And he walked forward to grasp cordially Philip's outstretched hand. Under these strange auspices, Philip met his old friend, and was presented to Mrs. Otis, who, even in the painful excitement of the moment, found herself wondering what Leigh saw to dislike in him.

"I must go back," exclaimed Leigh, impatiently. "I cannot bear it out here." And she turned towards the house. "O, if these people would only go away! How can they be so cruel? How can they stay and listen, when they care nothing for my poor little Gem!" And a flush of indignation passed over her pale face.

"They are not unkind," said Philip, pityingly. "It seems strange to us; but it is only their way. I think they are all sorry in their hearts, Miss Doane."

"Are they?" said Leigh, drearily. "I did not know; but I wish they would go away!" she repeated. Bessie seized her hand.

"Dear, come with us. You can do no good there, and you are worn out, and it is so hard for you."

"No, Bessie, I cannot."

"Let me drive you down with Bessie," begged Tom, affectionately, putting his hands on her shoulders and drawing her gently towards the waggon. "Please let me, Leigh."

"No, Tom," said Leigh, with the same immovable face.

"Perhaps I shall run away with you against your will," said Tom, trying to speak lightly. Leigh stepped to Bessie's side.

"Dear, I cannot talk now; but it is better for me to be with Gem. Tom, you do not know. You tell them," she said, turning to Philip; "you understand." And, putting her arms round Bessie's neck, she kissed her once, and, without another word, went swiftly back to the house. Tom looked very much as if he were going after her. In answer to his glance, Philip said:

"Better let her stay, Otis. She's about worn out, but one night more can't make much difference, I think Miss Doane meant that she found it harder to control herself away from Gem than with him, even if she can do nothing for him, did she not, Mrs. Otis?"

"Yes," said Bessie, sadly. "I wanted her to come with me, but it would be cruel to take her away, and you'll take care of her, Mr. Ogden, will you not?" she said, holding out her hand with a look full of confidence. "It is not like leaving her with strangers"; and she made a faint attempt to smile. "If you were not here, I could not leave her to go about with that poor pale face, and those great wild eyes." And the tears rolled down Bessie's cheeks. "I wouldn't be of the least use if I should stay, would I?"

"I think not, Mrs. Otis. No one can do anything but wait for the result. It must come soon. You may be sure I will not be neglectful of the trust you give me," he added, gratefully.

"You, of use? You look like it, you fluttering, tearful thing," said Tom to his wife, with mock fierceness. "The question is, Ogden, have I, or have I not, any marital authority? There are times of agony and despair, when tongue cannot express my suffering, and I am forced to respond, No, I have none whatever; but occasionally comes a moment like this,"—and without more ado he coolly lifted his wife into the waggon,—"which gives me strength and courage for the future."

Bessie smiled, but said, "O Tom!" reprovingly.

"I'm sorry for the boy in there," said he, "but I think so much hearse and funeral trappings entirely premature. I've heard of a woman who lived in a shroud, night and day, for twenty years,

When one would wear out she'd have another,—
the way my wife does with what she calls her
spring-suits,—but I'm inclined to regard things
more cheerfully, and I think that child will see
daylight yet."

"I think so, Tom," said Philip. "He's had a
tough time of it, but I have not been able to believe that this is the end of the bright little fellow."

"Ogden, let me know if I can be of any use. I
leave that wilful girl in your hands. Bring her
down to us if she faints. I hope everything will
come out all right."

"I hope and believe it will. This is Miss
Doane's 'happy Wednesday.' She was anticipating it with the utmost eagerness and delight,"
said Philip gravely. "However it may end I
shall bring her into the village early to-morrow
morning."

With an exchange of glances that said far more
than their words, the two men shook hands
warmly, and Tom drove off. Exhausted by the emotions she had experienced after the fatigue of the
day, and seeming still to hear the moans of the
child, Bessie silently leaned close to her husband.

"Poor little girl!" he said, the jesting tone quite
gone from his voice.

"Isn't it dreadful?" said Bessie, after some
moments. "And we expected so much! And our
poor Leigh looking like a ghost, and everything
so miserable! How hard it is to be happy in this
world!"

"What a Lady Macbeth she'd make!" said Tom,
deliberately ignoring her despondent tone. "She

had the horror in her eyes to perfection. If she had only rubbed her hands together. That was all that was wanting."

"Do you suppose it will ever be pleasant here? It seems to me I shall hear that child all my life."

"My dear, it is not an hilarious beginning, I admit, but I'll prophesy that Ogden will bring Leigh down, with good tidings, in the morning. The boy will get better; and if all Leigh says of him is true, you'll hear his voice in sounds a vast deal jollier than groans."

"But, dear, it is impossible to know surely."

"'We can't 'most always sometimes tell' much of anything in this world, but we won't bear any unnecessary burdens. I have a presentiment the little chap is going to get well," said he, stoutly. And Bessie was comforted by his cheery tones, as he meant she should be, in spite of herself.

When they arrived at the house he took her in his strong arms, and, carrying her up stairs like a child, deposited her in the big chair.

Bessie smiled at him.

"Tom, you are a good boy, if you are silly sometimes."

"You flatter me, upon my honour, you do, really."

"Tom, I want to tell you something."

"My ears are open," he said, as she hesitated.

"Leigh and Mr. Ogden," she began, "are— that is, they will be—I mean—I think so. Of course, one can't know certainly about such things, but still, Tom, I feel perfectly sure—yes, perfectly."

"I never was accused of being hypercritical, but I think I may say that I have, in the course of my life, listened to a more fluent and lucid announcement of a person's views," said Tom, gravely. "My dear, I would not presume to dictate, but would humbly suggest—as the old deacon said in his prayer—that you try that again."

"Why do you not understand, dear ? It's quite clear. Did you not notice her when she turned to him as she went away, and said, '*You* understand' ? "

"What if she did ? " Tom said bluntly. "That's nothing. He's been in the house with her three weeks. Of course he understands. Do you imagine it takes a man of Ogden's sense as long as that to see through a woman's whims ? "

"But, dear, she felt that he would understand her better than you or I. Better than I, her own sister. Is that nothing ? And did you not see the look in his eyes when he watched her as she went back to the house ? "

"I hope I have something better to do in this world than watching men's eyes, and ferreting out incipient love-affairs," laughed Tom.

"This is not an incipient love-affair, by any means," said Bessie, wisely.

"And you had time to discover all this in those few moments ? And that was why you smiled your prettiest, and made up to Ogden so tremendously, the minute you put your eyes on him ? O, these women ! " And Tom whistled.

"Dear, you exaggerate. I couldn't have smiled much. I was feeling too badly. And George

Eliot makes somebody say, 'She's not denyin' that women are foolish. God A'mighty made 'em to match the men.'" replied Bessie, triumphantly.

"And what does 'to match the men' mean? To be what we are not? A compliment? It strikes me that is the reasonable interpretation," chuckled Tom.

"Don't joke, Tom," said Bessie, solemnly.

"That's good. Pardon me for recriminating, but, if I mistake not, you began it this time."

"Never mind if I did, dear. How do you suppose little Gem is now?"

"Improving—improving rapidly," said Tom, with decision.

"Tom," said Bessie, after a moment's thought, "You may not think I know much, but there are some things which women always see quicker than men. You need not deny it, for men themselves admit it, and I know—I know," she repeated emphatically, "that Mr. Ogden is very much interested in Leigh."

"Can't a man look after a pretty girl as she walks off, without being spoony?"

"No; at least, not as Mr. Ogden looked; and 'spoony' is not a pretty word, my dear."

Tom took a plaster-of-paris image of "Praying Samuel" from the mantel, and eyed it reflectively.

"It is then your firm conviction, you small and sapient woman, that Ogden and Leigh will eventually—"

"Yes, dear, if you don't interfere."

"I? Why should I?"

"I do not mean that you would interpose any real objections and obstacles," said Bessie, with a smile; "but you must not tease Leigh."

"O, I must not, must I?" said Tom, wickedly.

"Not for a moment," replied Bessie, with great earnestness. "You see this is an extremely precarious affair. They have been quarrelling all the time. When two persons in their frame of mind quarrel and then 'make up,' as the children call it, it is lovely, perfectly lovely; but you must not say a word to Leigh. I wish *we* had quarrelled," she said, a little enviously. "It makes a courtship very much more brilliant."

Tom looked immensely amused.

"Nobody shall say I have not a chivalrous and lover-like soul. I'll quarrel with you to an unlimited extent. I'll show you heights of fine fighting such as you never dreamed of. Just say the word! When shall we begin?"

"O, it's not the same thing! It's not half so nice to quarrel now," she said, regretfully. "Tom, dear, the very nicest thing *now* is for you always to do exactly what I say. You promise to say nothing to Leigh?"

"I am to understand, then, that my lady approves of the match?"

"Yes — I think — I — do," said Bessie slowly. "I like him. I liked him at once; his voice and his face and his manner. And you like him so much, Tom, of course that influences me," she went on demurely. "You have told me so much about him, and you know you have most excellent judgment. Please promise, Tom," she said coaxingly.

"A man," began Tom in a tragic manner, "who can exist this amount of wheedling is a cynic ; nay, a misogynist, whom 'twere base flattery to call a villain." And striking an attitude, he looked up to imaginary galleries for applause. "I promise not to molest the two innocents. I swear it," he exclaimed in a sepulchral and stagy tone suggestive of slow music, blue fire, and fiends. "Now are you satisfied ? The sooner that tired head of yours is on its pillow the better. I am going down to the door for a smoke." Shortly after he called from the porch, "Bessie !"

"Hush, dear," she said, coming to the stairway. "Speak low, or you'll wake baby. What is it ?"

"Leigh's heaped-up vituperation of Ogden was all a hoax, feminine duplicity, was it ?"

"Not at all !" was the indignant response. "She was perfectly sincere. Can't a girl change her mind ?"

"I have heard it faintly intimated that she can," said Tom, dryly.

"Leigh disliked him extremely in the first place."

"Whew !" said Tom. "When do you suppose the wondrous change began ?"

"How do I know ? Why do you wish to work it out like a problem in geometry ? Men never do appreciate those fine points,"

"I presume not ; still, my dear, I think it is but fair to state, that while your assumption, with regard to our young friend may or may not be verified in the future, as yet I have seen no evidence that corroborates your views ; which are, to my mind, hasty, ill-formed, unfounded, and, need I add, essentially feminine."

"Tom, if you say another word in that heavy judicial style, I shall fall asleep here, standing on my feet. What you think or do not think upon this subject does not signify in the least. *I* do not think, I *know.* All you are to do is to behave, and await the result."

"Which I'm perfectly willing to do, It's Ogden's funeral, not mine, and either of them could do worse."

"And you'll be very good, and not trouble Leigh ?"

"Have I not promised, importunate being ?"

"Yes, Tom, you did," said Bessie, contritely. "1 know you'll be good. Good night, dear."

Tom sat and smoked until he heard Miss Phipps coming in the side entrance. He went out to meet her, and to ask how Gem was. As yet there was no change. He returned to the porch and his cigars. "The little fellow will pull through," he thought cheerily. "And we actually have stumbled upon a romance so soon, if my little wife is right, and I rather think she is. O, these women ! these women !"

CHAPTER XV.

"Pleasantly murmured the brook as they crossed the ford in the forest,
Pleased with the image that passed like a dream of love through its
    bosom,
Tremulous, floating in air, o'er the depths of the azure abysses,
Down through the golden leaves, the sun was pouring his splen-
    dours."

—LONGFELLOW.

"To hate the Devil and all his works is one thing. To say who is the
Devil and what are his works is another."—MISS THACKERAY.

"BUT you do not faint, Miss Doane, nor cry,
nor even look pale, nor fulfil in the slightest degree my preconceived theories with
regard to the way in which young ladies conduct
themselves after an excess of emotion."

"I should be sorry to seem impertinent, but do
you write for the magazines, Mr. Ogden? Except
in recent essays upon young women, I never met
with such extraordinary ideas as you advance. I
wonder if you can be in earnest. What do you
think of us any way?" And she turned her frank,
sunny face directly towards him. Her eyes looked
unnaturally large and bright, and her cheeks were
flushed crimson.

Philip glanced at her as she sat beside him in
the rumbling old waggon. What he thought of
young ladies as a class was one thing. What he
thought of her individually was another, and the
hour for telling her was not yet come.

L

"I did not know that young ladies could work as hard as you have worked for three weeks, crown it all by a night of extreme anxiety without one moment's sleep, and then look brilliantly happy at ' five o'clock in the morning.' "

"But everything looks happy and fresh and lovely. I never was so blessed in my life. Wasn't that the sweetest smile you ever saw that he gave me ? Wasn't it ? " she repeated eagerly.

Thus urged, Philip deceitfully assented, making, however, a mental reservation in favour of the smile which was then delighting his eyes.

"And then he went off into that lovely, quiet sleep ! Do hear those birds ! How glad they sound ! This air is simply intoxicating ! O Mr. Ogden, what if he should want me when he wakes !"

"He is too weak to want much of anything to-day ; but if he should want you by and by, you must let him want, Miss Doane. The danger is over, and Jane does wonders now, thanks to you, and I shall be there. I do not think he will miss you just yet."

"But he knew me. He looked directly at me. Why, you saw him ! He smiled, you know," she said with feverish haste.

"Indeed he did. He smiled directly at you, and at no one else, and you deserved that mark of favour. How changed the boy is ! He looks older, altogether different from the Jim I found when I came here."

"Gem was changed in many respects before his illness, from the mocking little mischievous elf who perched upon Miss Phipps's fence in the twilight

the first time I ever saw him, and seemed like a
bird of ill-omen because I felt so desolate. And
then he went flying and shrieking through the
gloom in the most astonishing manner. It was the
same evening," she began thoughtlessly, and then
stopped.

"Gem was improving wonderfully," said Philip,
coming quietly to her relief. "How did you manage it?"

"O, I did very little, I assure you! It was all
his own, dear, little bright self. I have not a bit
of a mission or a call or a sphere or an anything of
the sort. Gem has taught me more than I have
him, and has been of the greatest service to me in a
thousand ways. I think you did him good, Mr.
Ogden."

"I?" said Philip, in real surprise. "Not a bit
of it! I'm the last man in existence to go about
reforming his fellow-creatures," he went on with
some bitterness. "Miss Doane, I lead the most
selfish, aimless life in existence. No man ever was
of less use."

"Delightful!" exclaimed Leigh; "I always encourage sentiments of that kind. It is so seldom
one sees a man show the least humility, and when
he does, it is over so soon, and he immediately for-
gets that he ever knew the meaning of the word.
But, Mr. Ogden, you do preach, you know, sometimes," she said, laughing. "Gem told me about
the snail-sermon."

"And Gem told me about your anaconda lecture," Philip returned coolly.

"I hoped that he would tell, since I had the

pleasure of listening to a synopsis of your eloquent dissertation upon the 'chameleon,'" said Leigh, unabashed; but she changed the subject. "Did you lose all hope yesterday?"

"No, I think not. I was extremely anxious, but I did not quite give him up. Did you?"

"Not until those people came and listened, and then I really think I despaired of everything. They seemed so hideous and cruel and ghoulish. They made me frantic. I fairly hated them."

"I do not doubt it. You looked as if you did."

"How very difficult it is to be charitable to people whose ways one does not understand!" Leigh said, thoughtfully.

"Perhaps that is why I do fashionable girls such injustice," Philip said with a smile.

Leigh turned towards him quickly. "Mr. Ogden, I'm the happiest girl in the world this morning, and I think I'm tolerably amiable, but I shall grow savage in two minutes, if you begin to talk about 'fashionable girls,' like the magazines and newspapers."

"But I cannot, even for the pleasant little excitement of seeing you grow savage. My conversation is not up to the required standard of magazine articles or even newspapers, I'm afraid. But what is it that rouses your indignation?"

"I'm tired of reading and hearing about fashionable girls. What is a 'fashionable girl'? Do you know? Does anybody know?" Leigh went on impetuously. "People use the phrase as if it invariably meant shallow, empty-headed, and vain. I never could see that there was anything Christian in making one's self look dowdy. May not an unfashionable girl be silly ? Do we monopolize all the faults of the sex ? I suppose I'm a fashionable girl myself," she laughingly admitted, "so I speak with feeling. But why do people talk so ? "

" Perhaps because they have some reason. Perhaps because it is easier to write a clever and witty paper when one says ill-natured things. But, Miss Doane, do you believe that many of your young lady friends would have done what you have done down here in Edgecomb this summer ? You have a decided advantage in the argument, if I wished to take the opposite side. When a man knows that a young lady can walk her five miles easily, in all sorts of weather, with no apparent ill effect, he rapidly loses any foolish ideas he may have formed as to the universal delicacy of the sex ; and his past theories with regard to the inefficient, superficial ways of the modern ' girl ' must vanish when he sees a person so busy and helpful and practical as you have been. Are you sure you are not the Frau Bertha, the ' gentle white lady who steals softly to neglected cradles and rocks them ? ' My only refuge, you see, is to pronounce you an honourable exception. The froth exists, but you are not as fond of it as most girls."

" I am very sure I am not the Frau Bertha, for, according to the legend, she had an immensely large foot and a long iron nose," said Leigh, roguishly ; " and I do like froth. And, Mr. Ogden," she went on, with a vivid blush, " my friends would have done fewer foolish things than I, and the few things I may have done which are not foolish they would have done better."

"You do not seem fashionable at all, now," Philip said soberly.

"I do not take that as a compliment," laughed Leigh. "I am considered quite a fashionable person at home, I assure you. O, Mr. Ogden," she went on earnestly, "there is a great deal of injustice in it, really. People, sensible people too, do get so narrow in their way of looking at us. At a party, for instance, we are not expected to mention whether we made our dresses or not, or what good deeds we have performed during the day, nor to enumerate our several useful accomplishments, like the chorus of servants at the Richmond Fair in 'Martha.' We do not have the appearance of toiling and spinning, I admit, but that adds to the general effect. We look as finely as possible, —I always do, I assure you,—but, after all, we are not as we figure in the essays."

"You are eloquent, Miss Doane."

"No, I am not eloquent. But I never in any city met with the girls I find in the magazines and in some books. Sometimes, of course, I meet a young lady who seems stupid and shallow, but I cannot see that she is to blame if the Lord endowed her with less than the usual amount of common sense. If she were a chamber-maid, it would be the same. The fault lies deeper than in wearing pretty dresses. Mrs. Browning speaks of 'Vacuity trimmed with lace ;' but vacuity is vacuity, whether trimmed with lace or not. If a girl has little that is admirable or lovable in her nature, it

wouldn't remedy the difficulty if she should wear
cloth of frieze instead of cloth of gold. Now, our
set of girls at home,—would you really like to have
me tell you ? " she asked with a pretty hesitation.

" Indeed I would," Philp said heartily. " No
young lady ever talked to me as you are talking.
It is a very great pleasure to hear you."

Leigh went on rapidly. " We are not very profound, of course ; we are not particularly interested in protoplasm ; and when we come to Herbert
Spencer in our reading, we skip him, because we
think him appalling, but we study, more or less, all
of the time, and 'do' a little French and German quite
constantly, and we have our music,—most of us do
—and we read enough to have a faint idea of what
is going on in the world. Then, there are very
few girls who have no home duties. Some of my
friends always make their own dresses ; I never do,
I do not like to sew." And she looked at Philip as
if she expected to hear an exclamation of horror.
" Are you shocked ?"

" Not in the least. Your confession is quite a
relief to me. I always wondered how women could
possibly endure so much monotonous stitching.
And what else do you ? "

" O, little things ; yet each day seems full. We
are always busy. I do not think we ever feel that
we are frittering away our time, or that we are useless dolls, as we are popularly supposed to be. If
we all went as missionaries to the Fiji Islands, it
would be more to tell of ; but there are two sides
to every question, and Bessie would think I was a
heathen if I should leave her. I really do not

know the 'fashionable-girl' type at all, Mr. Ogden, except in isolated cases," she said, quite earnestly; "but I know very many sweet, bright
girls, who do not pretend to be wise or remarkable
in any way, but who do not dye their hair, nor
lace, nor pinch their feet, nor paint, and who are
just as true-hearted and womanly as if they did not
dance the German, and did not like to go to the
opera, and had not wealthy papas. Then we—we
fashionable butterflies, I mean—are not so feeble as
we are represented. Do not girls row and walk
miles and miles, and get brown and hardy and
healthy at hundreds of places on the coast every
summer? Where are people's eyes? Mr. Ogden,
it is impossible to tell anything about us," she
added, smiling brightly at him.   "A plain woman
is often vainer than a pretty one ; and the girl who
has the most languid and fashionable effect in a
whole roomful of girls may have sewed every stitch
in her elaborately made gown, and be a very efficient housekeeper, with a special talent for cooking.
And the girl with the ugly dress is not necessarily
the sweetest tempered. We are very uncertain,
but it is not fair to condemn us unheard. There
are really remote possibilities of good in us all," she
said, with comical gravity, "if we do not like the
idea of wearing a uniform of gray flannel, a straight
jacket, and a short plain skirt," she rather scornfully explained to Philip, "such as is urged strongly
upon us by the reformers, you know. I cannot feel
that I would be a better woman if I should wear
that costume, or anything else ugly and unbecoming
—green, for instance, which makes me look like a
fright."

"How intrepid you are, Miss Doane! This is a new development. I imagined that ladies never would admit that they were fond of dress."

"I like it hugely," Leigh said with emphasis. "I care for a beautiful colour and a graceful outline in dress as in anything else, and I like everything that is pretty and fresh and dainty. How can I help it? It is as instinctive

> 'As for grass to be green or skies to be blue;
> 'Tis the natural way of living.'

But I may not always. When I am forty-five, and have lost my friends and health and enthusiasm, and the world looks different, I may grow wise,— or morbid, I don't know which,—and take to writing essays, and denouncing pretty things, and advocating dull drab for universal wear, with never a gleam of rose-colour. I may even think it a crime to wear a locket, and a sleeve slightly open at the wrist an evidence of total depravity."

"*You* will never regard lockets and open sleeves in that light probably, Miss Doane, until you have an ugly arm and no locket."

"You are laughing at me. Perhaps I seem absurd to talk so."

"Certainly you do not. You are quite right, I think. And, right or wrong, you ought to have the privilege of expressing the feelings of your order."

"And that is the trouble," said Leigh, quickly. "Our order, as you call it, never does express itself. It is the target at which everybody shoots. When anything new and especially savage appears,

we girls at home hold indignation meetings. We
have sometimes been strongly tempted to issue a
'Round Robin.' Is not that what it is called
when ignorant people feel that they must protest
against injustice, and are not wise enough to do it
in any magnificent and striking way?" she asked
laughingly. "I really do not think that we are
unreasonable. We read with respect and interest
whatever physicians choose to write about us.
They speak what they do know and testify what
they have seen, and for our good. But why should
we be publicly denounced by our own sex? Why
should the purity of our motives be assailed, and
ideas of which we never dreamed imputed to us on
account of a ruffle, more or less, which to us
seems a non-essential? We fashionable girls think
that it is not kind or womanly to bring railing ac-
cusations against all persons who do not choose to
wear scant skirts, and whose opinions happen to
differ from our own, because we believe it is very
difficult to understand one another in this world,
where natures vary so much, and lives, and modes
of early training. We would rather keep our
hearts warm and charitable than to be able to write
the most trenchant anathemas against other women.
But in all human probability we shall continue to
be abused, and also to wear out pretty, fluttering,
frivolous ribbons to the end of time. And did you
ever, ever in all your life, listen to a lecture so
early in the morning? See that dear little squir-
rel! Isn't that bird-note almost too lovely? That
one that sounds so clearly above the rest, I mean.
O, Mr. Ogden, would you be so kind as to get me

a few of those ferns? They look so cool and
fresh, and Bessie would like to see them at breakfast. What a lovely, lovely world it is, now that
my Gem is better!"

As he stood on the edge of the wood, carefully
selecting the prettiest ferns, she said,—

" You must not notice how many foolish things
I say this morning, Mr. Ogden. I am not quite
responsible, you know. I imagine I am in a wild
state of delirium, and it is of small consequence to
me what I say, provided I can talk. Fortunately
for you, I shall soon have my family to afflict."

Philip did not tell her that if only he might
listen to the varying tones of her voice it was of
small consequence to him also what she said, nor
that he insanely wished that there were no family
waiting to receive her, but that they might go on
as they were forever, riding slowly through the
woods, with the freshness of the early morning
cooling their faces, the rosy clouds and golden light
of the sunrise before them, the joyous birds singing
in the branches over their heads, and the sweet
woody scents all around. Nor did he express any
of the other equally extravagant fancies that filled
his brain. It was not yet time, not yet, he constantly told himself, to risk the one thing in the
world most precious in his sight.

With the quiet manner she knew so well, he
said, passing her a great bunch of feathery ferns,
and getting in the waggon,—

" If I can only succeed in taking you safely to
your sister, I shall congratulate myself. You have
such a dazzling, unearthly effect this morning, I

have trembled all the way along lest you should vanish like a dryad into the heart of an oak ; and behind there, as we passed the spring, I held my breath, fearing that you would disappear, nixy-like, and leave me all alone, gazing sadly at a bubble. I am sorry to croak, but you show your fatigue in a queer way, and I fear you will feel it more, later. If you escape without an illness, I shall be surprised, and very happy," he added involuntarily. A pretty pleased light shone in Leigh's eyes, but she said quite carelessly,—

"O, I'm too contrary to be ill, because you and Tom expect it. I am excited, I know, and I cannot keep still. I am restless away from Gem. I am sure I should be better with him."

Philip shook his head doubtingly.

"But as he really does not need me, of course I shall go to Bessie for to-day."

"And go to sleep too, I hope."

"Indeed, no. I shall drink ever so many cups of coffee, in the first place. It is so fortunate you will not see me. You would be horrified."

"But I shall certainly stay to breakfast," Philip calmly announced, "if Mrs. Otis honours me with an invitation."

"Very well ; at your peril, then. I've given you fair warning. And, after the coffee, we shall go up to my sister's room, and Bessie and I will talk all day long, and discuss the details of the six weeks we have spent without each other, and Tom will be ridiculous, and I, to be honest, will be superhumanly silly. I always am after I have taken care of a sick person and lost a great deal of sleep.

I laugh immoderately at every thing for a day or two. Some people have headaches. I presume my silliness answers the same purpose."

Philip was in that ineffable state in which Leigh's silliness would seem more charming than the combined wisdom of the rest of the world; but he gave no sign, only said, as they stopped at Miss Phipps's gate,—

"May I come down to-night, report Gem's case, and see how you are ?"

" From curiosity to observe the condition I shall be in, after twelve hours of idiotic laughter ?"

" Perhaps; but may I come ?"

"Certainly; I shall depend upon hearing from Gem, and Tom will be very glad to see you," Leigh said sedately. "Actually, there's the dear boy up at this hour !" she exclaimed, as Tom rushed out of the house and down to the gate.

" How are you Ogden ? Leigh what's the matter with you ? Why do you 'twinkle, twinkle' ? I'm afraid of you."

" So am I, Tom. Is she not supernaturally brilliant ?"

" I think I must resemble a calcium light," Leigh said, laughing. " But, Tom, Tom, why do you not inquire about Gem ?"

" Because, Leigh, Leigh, I know about Gem," returned Tom, mockingly. " Why do you come home at this hour, with your inward joy dancing in your eyes, and burning in your cheeks, and illuminating the whole road like a phosphorescent glare in a bog, if Gem is not better ?"

" Should you consider ' phosphorescent glare ' a

compliment ?" inquired Leigh, gravely. " Do you
suppose he is trying to say that I am a 'sunshine in
a shady place'? It's only Tom, you know. He's
a little addicted to using large words which he does
not understand, but he means well."

" I think I would consider it said in a Pickwick-
ian sense, Miss Doane. Tom, how do you happen
to be awake? Five o'clock was not of old, me-
thinks, your hour of rising?"

" My wife's evil conscience roused her, although
she says that it was anxiety about Leigh, and the
consciousness of being in a strange place ; and she
had no mercy, but cruelly sacrificed my morning
nap to her selfishness. Ogden, you'll take breakfast with us, of course?"

" My sister will be extremely happy to have you,"
said Leigh, cordially.

" I shall be glad to stay, on every account," replied Philip, " but particularly because Miss Doane
has promised me the pleasure of seeing her get intoxicated on coffee."

" If you knew her as well as I do," said Tom,
" you'd grow hardened and indifferent to all her
wicked ways." And he smiled affectionately at the
girl, who made in return a mocking little face at
him ; and, telling the gentlemen she would give
them an opportunity to abuse her at their pleasure,
she ran up to Bessie.

Rapidly and joyously the sisters talked, and all
the gloom of the day before vanished speedily in
the fresh fair morning. Bessie eagerly asked
question after question, about Gem, and Leigh as
eagerly answered.

"Go to the ant, thou sluggard, and be wise," chanted Tom's mellow baritone. "Come down, you magpies."

"In a moment, my dear," was the response. "Leigh's hair!" Bessie whispered mysteriously as he came up to expedite matters.

"And don't I know about Leigh's hair in every possible state, and hasn't Ogden seen it flying at loose ends in a very dishevelled and disgraceful condition? What's the use of beautifying it now? Too late, my dear, too late! The mischief's done."

"O, run down, Tom, do, please! It's not polite to leave Mr. Ogden."

Tom went down.

Presently he shouted,—

"Bessie!"

An animated conversation was going on above. He received no response.

"E-liz-a-beth!"

This was successful. Bessie and Leigh descended the stairs together.

"Good morning, Mr. Ogden. I am so pleased you will stay with us, and so grateful to you for bringing my sister back," said Bessie warmly; and, extending her hand to Philip, took his arm, and led the way into the breakfast-room.

Tom and Leigh followed, the former wearing a curious and amused expression as he observed the extreme graciousness of his wife's greeting. So soon as they were seated, forgetful of, or deliberately disregarding his vow, he asked in a soft and scrupulously polite voice, which Leigh and Bessie knew invariably meant mischief,—

" Is it the custom in Edgecomb for young people to take their pleasure drives at sun-rise ? Charmingly invigorating habit, is it not, Ogden ? Such freshness everywhere, such joy, such a roseate hue over everything, is there not, Leigh ? Why, Bessie," he asked, looking round with would-be innocent eyes, "what are you nudging me with your foot under the table for ? Does anybody know what I've done ? Have I said anything ? "

" You never saw a sunrise before, I imagine, Tom. It seems to have had a singularly bad effect upon you. I wouldn't try it again," Philip said carelessly.

Leigh devoted herself to her coffee ; and Tom, having received a volley of warning, beseeching, threatening glances from his wife, postponed his attack until a more favourable season ; and soon everybody began to discuss Gem with enthusiasm.

When this small skeleton, wickedly summoned by Tom, had been thrust out of sight, the early breakfast was a merry occasion for each of the four. The tall ferns nodded gracefully in the centre of the table. Never was coffee so strong and fragrant. Never did rolls wear so inviting a brown. Never were berries so ripe and juicy. Phipps's features were observed more than once to relax their rigidity.

It was already whispered that Tom was evidently her favourite among her guests, and many a well-turned compliment did that wily youth express whenever she was within hearing.

" How can you talk about feminine arts, you base deceiver ? " said Leigh.

" Bread is the staff of life, my child, and Phipps makes my bread. Uncommonly good bread it is, too. Why, then, should I not strive to strengthen the bond which already exists between her soul and mine ? Besides, I admire her immensely," he added with irresistible solemnity.

And Miss Phipps, coming into the room at that moment with hot rolls, little dreamed what was the cause of the extreme jollity in which these curious young persons were indulging.

Her inward comment was, " Never see sech goin's-on sence I was born into this world, never ! To say nothin' o' them brakes stuck up kinder pert-like amongst the victuals ! "

M

CHAPTER XVI.

" He looked at her as a lover can ;
She looked at him, as one who awakes,—
The past was a sleep, and her life began."
                                        BROWNING.

"COME, my little dears ! We cannot stay here star-gazing forever. That fragile flower is drooping," said Tom, pointing to Leigh. Upon a pile of planks, lying conveniently upon the old pier, which jutted out from the middle of the bridge, Leigh sat at Bessie's feet, leaning her head languidly against her sister's knee. Philip thought how pale and sweet both faces looked in the half light, and Tom paced up and down before the group with his cigar. The day which had begun for Leigh with the joyous sunrise ride, and which she and Bessie had passed lazily under the trees on the lawn, or cozily in the deep window-seats, was ending in quiet happiness down on the old bridge in the starlight. Edgecomb and the line of the Romney hills lay in shadow, the water glistened before their eyes, a little new moon shone faintly in the western sky, the strong salt air blew refreshingly towards them.

" Come, children ! " repeated Tom. " Leigh, are you going to condescend to sleep to-night, or shall you sit bolt upright, with your eyes propped open ? No one knows, Philip, how I've laboured to-day to make that obstinate girl close her lovely eyelids; but my sweetest lullaby failed to move her."

" Mr. Ogden, I wish you might have heard what Tom calls his lullaby," said Bessie. " It was a series of direct questions which lasted from morning until you came to us, just in season, I think, to save Leigh's tottering reason."

" And every question," put in Leigh pathetically, " related to me,—my words, my ways, my personal appearance. However interesting one may be to one's self, there is such a thing as holding a mirror too long before one's face."

Tom chuckled as they discoursed upon his misdeeds. It was all quite true his harrowing conduct that day would have effectually murdered sleep in the drowsiest mortal. He had received a merited reproof from Bessie for having dared to perjure himself so shamelessly at breakfast, and had been peremptorily forbidden to again approach the delicate ground upon which, according to her, Leigh and Philip were standing. Debarred thus from his natural prey, he was forced to solace himself with such small game as came in his path, and he questioned Leigh remorselessly as to why her " cheek's pale opal glowed with a red and restless spark," and why were her eyes so big and yellow, and would she minutely describe her symptoms, and why did she hop about so strangely, and why did she do a dozen different things in as many minutes, and so on *ad infinitum.*

" Don't you believe their malicious slanders, Ogden. Imagine a man of genius, like me, mewed up in a country town with these two chattering girls. I was forced, in self-defence, to make a study of Miss Doane. Dull ignorance, cannot, of course, sympathize with the investigations of the scientific mind," remarked Tom, with a graceful wave of his hand, and throwing his cigar into the water. "Leigh's case is one of peculiar interest, I shall instantly resume my subtle analysis,—you understand, young women!—if I cannot immediately prevail upon you to abandon that very picturesque attitude and those boards."

At this threat they rose reluctantly, and stood for a moment looking off over the water.

"It's a pity to go," said Bessie with a sigh.

"It is so pretty, and it will never look the same again."

"It is likely to look better before it looks worse," said Tom in a hearty and unsentimental manner.

"Which is a good, comfortable theory, Tom, but it does not always work well," added Philip.

> "'Nothing can be as it has been before.
> Better so call it, only not the same.'"

quoted Leigh softly. And they turned away and walked slowly along the bridge towards home, Leigh and Philip fell a little behind. They talked together quietly, as old friends, rejoiced in Gem's safety, planned pleasant surprises for his convalescence. They discussed the time of the probable appearance of Idlewild.

"I hope you will have the happiest trip imaginable," said Philip, "and get thoroughly rested. With Tom and Blake you can't fail to be very jolly,"

Why did he not say " we," Leigh asked herself. Was he not going too ? The question almost passed her lips, but something withheld it. Bessie and Tom were leaning over the railing of the bridge, a short distance from them. They too stopped, and stood in silence looking at the familiar outlines. There lay the fort. Each remembered that gray morning, ages ago, it seemed now, when they had hated each other so cordially. Far below, over the glistening water, rose Birch Point. How pretty and spirited she had looked that day, Philip thought. Leigh remembered that she had said to herself,

> " It was the boatmon Ronsalee,
> And he sailed through the mists so white."

as Philip pulled into the cove so easily that day. How lovely it was, with the western light shining on the water, and bringing out so strongly the different shades of green in the woods on the opposite shore ! And the swift wherry, darting in suddenly, had not injured the picturesque effect, nor had the figure in the boat been deficient in manly grace and strength, nor had the cordial, pleasant voice that had responded to Gem's summons jarred upon her. Had she liked him a little even then, this friend whose presence was so restful now that the summer was almost gone ? And he was not going with them in the yacht ? Perhaps they might not see him when they returned. What did he really mean, she wondered. Leigh felt troubled, confused, but of one thing she was almost sure, that now, as they stood quietly in the starlight, was the time, the very last time she might ever have, possibly, to thank him for all that he had done, and to speak with perfect frankness of their first acquaintance. Still she hesitated. She had been silent so long, it was difficult to speak now. Yet why not? Why wait a moment longer? There were Bessie and Tom, She had only deferred speaking until they should be here. Now was the opportunity. "To-morrow, who can tell? The Idlewild might come in, and all would be excitement and hurry and confusion, and she might go away with never an honest word of apology, and leave Mr. Ogden to think she was ungenerous, ungrateful. She glanced up at him. His face was dark and thoughtful, as he stood erect, looking straight beyond him. How very, very hard it was for her to begin! She leaned over the railing, and tried to see a fish which had just leaped and stirred the water.

"Miss Leigh, shall we not go on?" said Philip. "If you were in your usual condition, I would beg you to stay; but I don't like to keep you out this evening, even with my man's selfishness, as you call it."

"You do not keep me," said Leigh. His voice had given her courage. "I wish to stay, for I have something to say to you, and I may not see much of you after this." Philip started, and watched her closely. "I wish to tell you," she went on simply, but without looking up at him, "that I am very sorry I was so rude and foolish, and received you in such an inexcusable way at the fort. I thought then I had some reason. I

think, now, I had none." she continued rapidly, as
Philip was about to speak. " Please let me finish.
I only want you to know how good you've been
to me, and with what kindness and courtesy and
generosity you've repaid me for all my rudeness,
and I am very sorry for everything—everything,"
she repeated ; " and if you can forgive me—"

" I beg you will not say another word," said
Philip, in a low, hurried voice, taking both her
hands in his impetuously, and holding them in a
firm grasp. " You pain me by talking so. Why
should you say 'forgive' to me ? I have nothing
to forgive,—nothing whatever. It is my place to
beg for pardon at your feet,—for pardon and for
more, for more, my darling—Leigh, do you not
know—"

" Ah, don't !" said Leigh, turning away, and
burying her face in her hands. His manner, his
eager words, the strange new depths in his voice,
were a revelation to her. The tenderness which
had often sounded in his tones she had accepted
unconsciously, or construed into simple kindness
to her and Gem. This passionate voice was a different thing. She could not understand its meaning, nor that of the face which was looking directly
into her own. She was inexpressibly weary in mind
and body. Her fatigue and excitement, followed
by the long quiet evening, were at last telling
strongly upon her, and sending a penetrating languor
over her whole system. Never, perhaps, in her
life, had she been so utterly unnerved as she was,
even before Philip had spoken, and what he had
said seemed too much for her to bear. Not once

had she thought of this quiet, watchful friend as a lover. She had done him a wrong. He had been good to her. She wished to make reparation, and to thank him, before their lives, thrown together so curiously for a time, should separate for ever. She wished him to say he forgave her, in the old friendly way. This new voice had sounded too suddenly in her ears. She was too tired to listen to its throbbing, restless, seeking tones. Instinctively she had lifted her hand as if to shield herself from a blow, and shrinking, troubled, pleading, had said,—

"Ah! don't, don't, please!"

In an instant the old quiet returned to Philip's manner. He had waited long, it seemed to him. He could wait longer. The sweet friendliness of her manner, as she offered her frank apology, he had not misunderstood, or estimated for more than it was worth, yet it seemed that he had spoken too soon. Would she ever learn not to dislike him? Suddenly, as he looked down upon her half-averted face, a true appreciation of Leigh's position dawned upon him,—

"Because where reason even finds no flaw,
Unerring a lover's instinct may,"—

and his heart was filled with a pitying tenderness.

"I am a brute to give her one more thought. She is no more fit to hear me than a tired child. It would be ungenerous to distress her by saying more." Yet Philip found it almost beyond his strength to reason and wait when his very life seemed trembling in the balance. He craved an answer, even if it were that she cared not for him. Her weariness, the pale, sad face from which all the sparkle had gone, moved him deeply; and a wild impulse to take the drooping figure in his arms, and draw that weary head to his heart, seized him. He set his teeth together, turned and looked away from Leigh, following with his eye the long, dark line of the bridge, steadied himself manfully, and in a moment said in his ordinary manner,—

"Shall we go on now, Miss Leigh? Tom and your sister have just started, I believe." She took his proffered arm, and they resumed their walk.

"You are very good," she said gratefully, when they had gone on some moments in silence. "I did not mean—I did not know," she went on brokenly; then, not even making an effort to complete her sentence, said simply, "I'm very tired."

"Yes, I know," Philip replied gently. "Forgive me for troubling you. We are only Gem's two friends now. He is not quite well yet, and I may still claim you as my friend, for his sake, may I not?" This light appeal, and the old jesting tone poor tired Leigh found that she could answer without too much perturbation.

"I think perhaps we are friends for our own sakes, through Gem, of course, but—" She hesitated; her words were still refractory; they would not come at her bidding.

"Bless the boy!" exclaimed Philip, emphatically; and Leigh looked up and met his smile. Was it a dream, then, this scene of a few moments before? This was not the same man. It was only the old Philip, whose presence gave her rest and relief. They said little as they passed up the village street. Leigh's brain was whirling, yet she felt too fatigued to really think; and Philip, in spite of the little repelling gesture with which she had received his avowal—in spite of her begging him to say no more—could not feel like a hopeless and despondent lover. The intuition of love had taught him why she had repulsed him. He did not think she loved him, but she had shown him that she trusted him. She had said that they were friends. Perhaps a long, long patience would accomplish the rest. Such, as they crossed the common, were his thoughts, which were interrupted by Tom's jovial voice in advance.

" Leigh, if you're quoting poetry, mind your cæsu-ras," he called out in a pedantic and warning manner.

" Miss Doane is too tired to trouble herself about trifles," retorted Philip.

" And who made him Leigh's champion ?" muttered Tom. " Things must be advancing rapidly, when that ready tongue of hers yields its right of retort."

" Did I not tell you so ?" asked Bessie in triumph. " But, Tom"—reproachfully—" how could you have said that to Leigh ? Do you not know you might have intruded your *cæsuras* at a most interesting and critical moment ?"

" And have I not received explicit instruction not to appear as if I imagined there could by any possibility be an interesting moment in the career of those young persons ? In that state of sublime ignorance which you demand of me, what was more natural than my charming and facetious remark? Hard as I strive to please you, I seem to fail in every particular."

"Of course you do, because you are an incorrigible, teasing boy," she replied, giving a scornful emphasis to the last word.

"May I not turn round and ask Leigh if she observes how strangely brilliant Venus is to-night?" he meekly asked.

"Indeed you may not," Bessie replied severely.

"Well, what do you suppose they are talking about?" continued the wicked Tom. "They keep me in awful suspense. Why do they pause so long upon the brink of the Rubicon? *I* could help them over. Mayn't I, Bessie?"

"Hush, Tom!" putting her hand over his lips as he was about to speak. "You'd be more apt to help them in and drown them," she whispered, as Leigh and Philip joined them.

One moment more Philip had alone with Leigh that evening. Bessie had disappeared in search of wine, which she insisted Leigh must have, and Tom had followed, and their two laughing voices could be heard above as they unpacked a hamper.

"Miss Leigh, forgive me if I trouble you, but I have so much to say to you. May I say one little word more?"

"Of course you may say what you like, Mr. Ogden. I am not entitled to so much consideration. I am tired, you know, and stupid," she said, putting her hand to her head wearily; "but I am not *in extremis.* I can listen when a friend speaks."

And Leigh smiled at him from the window-seat, as he stood before her.

"It is only this," he said hurriedly. "Pardon me for saying it now, but I may not have another opportunity. I made arrangements a few weeks ago to join a party of friends who are fishing at Manhegan, instead of going on the Idlewild trip. I thought my presence would not be agreeable to you. I did not wonder at that," he added, meeting Leigh's regretful, deprecating glance. "You see I thought, even after the amicable relations we had assumed 'for Gem's sake,' some unlucky reminiscence would continually pop up and disturb your peace, and I concluded it would be altogether better if I should not go with you."

"You were extremely thoughtful," said Leigh, quietly, turning away, and, with face pressed close against the pane, peering out into the darkness.

"But now I feel differently. I regret that I have agreed to go to Manhegan. I have been due there some days, but could not, of course, leave Gem." He paused, then went on, growing more earnest and rapid every moment. "Lately I have dared to hope that my presence on the yacht might not drive away all your pleasure. Leigh, I have not thought it, I have only hoped, and I have even dared to tell myself that possibly you would allow me to join the party later at some place where the yacht puts in." Leigh listened silently, but did not turn her head. "Do not misunderstand me. I am asking nothing of you. You pledge yourself to nothing. It is simply your permission to see you again—to receive from you a friend's welcome

—only that." And his voice pleaded so earnestly that again he held himself back, and said, "Forgive me—try to forgive me—I am presuming again upon your patience. You need not answer a word to-night," he said, as Leigh turned towards him. "I have no right to distress you. Yet how can I be wholly silent?" he exclaimed, impetuously.

Leigh rose from the window-seat, and stood before him. There may have been a little quiver about the sensitive mouth, and her clasped hands were pressed closely together, but she spoke calmly.

"Mr. Ogden, I cannot of course, fail to understand you. Pardon me if I was cowardly and childish on the bridge just now. You have a right to speak and be answered. You startled me; and you give me much to think of,—far, far too much for me to answer now." Here she faltered a little; then, regaining her composure, "Yet I would like you to know that I think you are very, very good to me, and such goodness as yours demands in return fair, honest treatment at least." Looking earnestly into Philip's eager face, she said "You say I pledge myself to nothing by what I say now?"

"Absolutely nothing."

"I am glad," Leigh said simply. "I could not promise anything. I do not know."

"You need not promise, and you need not know."

"Then, Mr. Ogden," slowly, and with grave, sweet dignity, "I would be pleased if you were to go with us on the Idlewild; and if you care to join us by and by, I will give you the friend's welcome. I think I will not wait for my sister. Good night, Mr. Ogden."

Reverentially, as if she were a young princess, Philip lifted to his lips the hand she extended to him, thus silently expressed his gratitude.

Afterwards he and Tom sat smoking together at the door.

" Tom," said Philip deliberately between his puffs, " have you anything to say against me,— my moral character, temper, position, business prospects ? "

Tom turned squarely round, looked Philip in the face, and said,—

" Can't say that I have."

" ' Speak now, or forever after hold your peace.' "

" Hm ! as far along as that ? Do you want to shake hands, Ogden ? "

" Wait, Tom. I don't wish to take your hand under false pretences. I am addressing you formally, now, as Miss Doane's natural protector, and announcing my intentions simply. What hers may be is different matter."

" My dear Philip, as Miss Doane's guardian, then, I give you my hearty approval and sympathy ; and, as a keen observer of the fair sex, I feel justified in assuring you that there can be no reasonable doubt of a delightful unanimity of sentiment between you." Philip smiled, and quietly replied,—

" The matter rests with Miss Doane, Tom. It is out of my hands. I wait her decision."

The two young men smoked on in silence.

" Brother ! embrace me ! " burst forth from the irrepressible Tom.

" Excuse me," said Philip, laughing. " The relationship is horribly premature, and as for the demonstration, I shouldn't enjoy it."

" Will you shake hands, then ? "

" With pleasure." And each took the other's hand, with that strong, long grasp in which men, deeming words at such moments a meaningless form, express hearty good-will, affection, it may be. Behind Tom's jesting manner his honest soul looked out and wished his friend goodspeed ; and Philip saw it, thanked him in his heart, and went off down the road to the cottage at a rapid, swinging gait, with hopeful, happy fancies thronging in his mind, all created by "the might of one fair face."

CHAPTER XVII.

" To say why girls act so or so,
Or don't, 'ould be presumin'.
Mebby to mean yes and say no
Comes nateral to women."
　　　　　　　LOWELL.

" Heart, are ye yet great enough
For a love that never tires ? "
　　　　　　　TENNYSON.

A WEEK passed. Gem steadily improved.
and each day Leigh sat with him, told
stories, sang to him, and made the long
hours seem shorter to the restless, impatient child.
Bessie came, too, and Gem, although at first a little
shy with her—for his illness had changed him somewhat—soon grew to watch for her coming also, and
to welcome " Miss Leigh's Bessie," who was " like
Miss Leigh an' yet she warn't, an' talked like Miss
Leigh and yet she didn't."　Tom fussed and fumed,
and declared that he was dying of neglect, and that
he had heard nothing but " Gem this and Gem
that " since he came ; yet evidence of his warm interest was not wanting at the boy's bedside.　One
day he brought out some choice wine, with a stern,
" Take that to yon pampered fledgling."　And
curious wooden puzzles, just light enough for small,
weak fingers to play with, and not too intricate for
the little brain, wearied by long illness, to solve,
appeared mysteriously in baskets of fruit and
flowers which Bessie sent to Gem.

Philip was much with Tom, and saw little of Leigh during the few days he remained in Edgecomb. He had long talks with Gem when Leigh was not at the cottage. When she would enter the room, he would resign his place near the invalid, and, after a friendly word or two, go out. His manner was as of old during Gem's illness. They two were Gem's friends simply. He was quietly waiting, giving her time, making no allusion to the deeper waters they had entered. Only once, and then just before his departure he said.—

" I shall go to Manhegan to-morrow. I still have your permission to join the Idlewild party ? "

" Yes, if you can find us," she answered gayly. " From all I can hear, I imagine we are going to be a very erratic band of voyagers, and you, in search of us, may go flying by some little harbour where we are safely at anchor all the time."

" I think I shall be able to find you without much difficulty," Philip returned with a smile. " The coast of Maine will give us an extended field for a game of hide-and-seek. You will not escape me, unless you do it wilfully."

" I promise to ' play fair.' "

" Thank you. Then I shall certainly find you somewhere."

' " Somewhere, somewhen, somehow,' as it says in ' Water Babies,' added Leigh, laughing. " Delightfully vague is it not ? Good bye, then, Mr. Ogden. I wish you a charming time, and ever so many fish at Manhegan. You must bring us some stories from the rocky wild old place. the fishermen there ought to be wonderfully interesting."

N

" I'll try and pick up something worth repeating. Every new idea I gain is of enormous value to me, as my mind only dwells upon events which have occurred since Gem's illness," Philip said, with a curious smile. And, though the good-bye was spoken, he still lingered. " My previous history is a blank."

"Perhaps it would be well for both of us to bury a few weeks in oblivion," said Leigh demurely. " I am sure when I view myself in certain lights, I am not an edifying spectacle. It was all very ridiculous, was it not ? But I'm sorry ; and Mr. Ogden," she went on roguishly, " if it will afford you any pleasure, you may break my poor umbrella into a thousand pieces, although Tom did bring it to me from London, and my affections still cling to it, in spite of its depravity. And you may burn that foolish sketch-book, with solemn and appropriate rites," she went on merrily. " And can I give you satisfaction in any other way ? "

" You know perfectly well that you can," was the low response.

Philip had not intended to urge his suit as he bade her farewell for a few days. He had contemplated a cool and unsentimental leave-taking, as a sort of sanitary measure, which would benefit him in the end. He saw that Leigh was not quite sure of herself, nor did he wonder at all that she wanted time to think. He looked forward with a firm, patient hope to the day when he could gain her love. He felt in some way assured that that day would surely come. If Leigh had not some little regard—affection, it may be—for him, he reflected, with a wondering thankfulness, if it would be impossible for her to care for him as he wished her to care, she would have known it at once, and would have told him so in frank womanly words. Their present intercourse, which outwardly resembled the calm ease of a long friendship, would have been impossible, had he been an uncertain aspirant for higher honours. Gem was still the connecting link, and there were all the curious and familiar elements of life among the Holbrooks, which made it, to a certain extent, natural that they should fall back into the old grooves ; yet beneath this surface life was the deep undertone. She had given him encouragement, and he was showing her plainly, that, so long as she needed, she might rely on his patience and delicate consideration for her doubts. He understood her far better than Leigh imagined. She was not a girl who was in a chronic state of listening breathless expectation of a proposal of marriage from every eligible man she met. He had watched her very closely. He had seen that she would greet him with sweet, pleased eyes, when he would join her, after an absence of some hours ; yet he had also seen that her welcome, while it evinced trust and sympathy, was too frank to lie very far below the surface. He knew that his little attentions, his constant care of her, she had accepted all along, as she, with her honest, innocent heart, could not have done, had she not felt a real liking for him ; yet it had been only a liking, Philip saw. Why should it grow in one moment into a great resistless love like his own. True love is by turns humble and proud. Philip was in the stages of humility. "Any sweet, good woman is too good for the best man that walks the earth," he said to himself. And why should this rare Leigh, this priceless pearl of women, "so purer than the purest," be his at once for asking? He could wait, for he knew well its fair radiance was destined to shine into his life. Why, then, with so dear and blessed a hope, should he not be patient? So he reasoned; yet, as Leigh had looked up at him, and carelessly asked if there was any other way in which she could give him satisfaction, involuntarily had answered with his whole soul in his voice, and he the tone and word could not be recalled.

Leigh stood leaning against one of the pillars which supported Miss Phipps's "antique portico," with the light from the hall streaming out upon her face.

The usual group of four had been chatting out in the porch, but Bessie had judiciously departed, dragging away with her the reluctant Tom, and calmly announcing a palpably improbable reason for withdrawing.

Tom feelingly remonstrated,—

"If you will persist in being general of this army, Bessie, I wish you might become a more profound tactician; and I must protest against a wife of mine making such unblushingly mendacious assertions. That last was too painfully attenuated, —the very fibbiest of fibs."

"Tom," Bessie said, oracularly, "Mr. Ogden is going away. Everything depends upon what is done at this moment. Farewells are extremely important."

"Why do you not write a book ? 'Love-Making Made Easy' would attract attention, and I never, in all my life, met anybody who knew quite so much about it as you do."

"Who taught me, I'd like to know !" was the pert and pointed rejoinder.

"I'm sure I can't imagine," retorted Tom, with a reflective air. "Let me think. Barton, wasn't it, or Nettleton, or Allen, or some other one of those dandy fellows, who were always spinning about you until I appeared," he went on with a magnificent flourish, "and they vanished like dew before the sun. Yet, what I did in those old and halcyon days, my beloved, I accomplished by my own unaided genius. No one ever spread cotton-wool in my path as you do in Ogden's," he murmured plaintively. "And Leigh, too,—it was not ever thus. She was not once so brittle. Will she really break if I touch her ?"

"Tom, you know you are quite as much interested as I am, only you are too ridiculous to acknowledge it."

"Interested ? Of course I am, only I don't want to be harassed and hampered, and prevented from showing my interest in my own peculiar and pleasing method. A pretty way to evince interest it is to rush off into the dining-room and close two doors behind one, so one cannot possibly hear what is going on. I want to hear, I tell you ! I want to be on the spot. Why do you restrain me, you cruel woman ? I want to give Ogden an encouraging pat on the back, and charm Leigh with my *naïveté* and innocent prattle !"

"O Tom, do be quiet!" said Bessie, stifling with laughter. "You grow worse and worse. They will certainly hear you."

"I wish they would. It might hurry up the final tableau. Sweet thing!" he exclaimed, rolling his eyes. "Can't you see it, Bessie? Ogden and Leigh joining hands just before the foot-lights, and bowing gracefully to the audience. I, at stage right, doing the heavy walking-gentleman to perfection, the tearful old paternal, the 'bless you, my children,' style of thing, you know, while a smile of righteous joy will play over my mobile features, and

'How pleasant is Saturday night,
When we've tried all the week to be good,'

will emanate from my whole presence, and—"

"That's more than enough about you, you egotistical, conceited creature! Where will I be, if you please, sir?"

"You? You will play watchful, protecting spirit then, as you do now, my angel. You will be 'the sweet little cherub that sits up aloft,' at the extreme top of the stage left. You will wear spangled tarlatan, a gilt-paper crown, and a delicious smirk; and your exquisite arms, to which will be attached gorgeous pink calico wings, will dreamily wave, and fling down benisons upon the happy pair, while the supernumerary will burn beautiful yellow and green light at the wings, and the badly tuned violins will wail, and the curtain will fall amid tumultuous applause."

"Tom, I do not think I can tolerate such a

scene as this even in joke, and from you. Who ever heard of an angel in pink ? "

" And should not the angel of love appear in rose-colour ? "

" And yellow and green lights ! Your description is abominable, and highly improper, too, being strangely suggestive of Black Crook transformation scenes."

While they talked thus after their usual fashion in the dining-room, where Bessie had caged her husband, out at the porch a conversation of different import was going on.

Philip had spoken again.

" You know perfectly well that you can," he had said. " My life is in your hands."

Leigh's heart beat fast, and she nervously pulled in pieces a honeysuckle-blossom, sacrificing the fragrant, unoffending flower in her troubled mood.

" Mr. Ogden, may I speak very frankly to you ? I think there should be no disguise between us, whatever may come, and I know you will not misunderstand me ; and you will pardon me if what I am about to say seems strange ? "

" Do not hesitate to say anything you wish. I cannot misunderstand."

" In all these days in which you have been so good, and have given me time to think, it seems to me I ought to feel sure of myself, and I am not, Mr. Ogden. I am so sorry, but I feel troubled, full of doubt."

" Why should you feel so ? It is no light thing, I ask of you," Philip said gently. Then, after a moment, " Could you tell me what especially makes you troubled ? "

"I would like to tell you if I can. I wish to show you what is in my heart. It seems to me the only way," she hesitated. Again the innocent honeysuckle-vine suffered, as Leigh's unconscious hands ruthlessly showered leaf and flower upon the steps. Abruptly she began. "Mr. Ogden, it is so different from my theories. All girls have theories, you know. I cannot deny that I care for you more than I cared for any one before," she said slowly, and so low, that Philip scarcely heard the words that were so dear to him. "Wait," she went on, with a little imperious gesture, as Philip eagerly began to speak,— "wait. I care for you more, but how can I be sure that I care for you enough? How can I?" And the earnestness of her voice deepened as she repeated her question, and looked straight into the eyes of the man that loved her. "You have been good to me. You have cared for me constantly in little kind ways. Mrs. Browning says, 'these things have their weight with girls'"; and a faint smile trembled about Leigh's lips. "I suppose she knew. You have been with me weeks and weeks. I have grown used to you, and now you tell me that you love me; and in return I give much regard, a grateful affection perhaps, but is it love? It is not like the love I have dreamed of!" she exclaimed passionately.

Philip wondered if there were another woman in the world so true as the one who stood before him, trying to let him read her very heart as if it were an open book, and whose face and attitude and voice, by sudden eloquent little changes each moment, seemed to reveal every phase of the feeling which stirred her so deeply.

He did not speak, for he saw that she had more to say to him.

"Let me speak more plainly." And she carefully chose her words, and endeavoured to be quite calm. "Your presence makes me very happy. I think I would like you to come very often to my sister's home, yet I do not feel that for you I would, if you asked me to-day, give up that home and all the pleasant things in my old life," Leigh went on bravely, though she was evidently making a mighty effort. "I have always believed no woman ought to marry a man if she feels she can under any circumstances be happy without him. Am I talking strangely? Forgive me. Do not be angry with me. I do care very much for you, and I should miss you if you did not come to my home, and I should think of you often at first, but after a time I think I might be quite happy without you." Then, with a tremulous voice, suggestive of the deepest emotion, and also of a nervous desire to laugh, she said, "A woman, if she really loves a man, ought to be willing to go and live in a log-cabin with him, out on the prairies, and I do not love you enough for that. I know I do not. Do you think me speaking lightly," she said, pleadingly. "It is so hard to tell you exactly what I mean, and I am so .sad at heart. But when you offer me so royal a gift as your love, when you place all that you have, and all that you are, at my feet, I must, at least give you absolute truth in return. You see how I trust you. I am trying to tell you every thought."

"I know that you trust me," Philip said, taking in his own her two trembling hands, and holding them firmly, " and I believe that I can teach you to love me. Leigh, you must love me a little, or you could not let me hold these dear hands in mine, nor touch them with my lips. See, I kiss them over and over, and you do not draw them away. Already you give me far more than I deserve, and for the rest I can wait very, very patiently."

Leigh was touched indescribably by the quiet tenderness of his manner.

" But," she said, " is this right? What if the day comes when I look you in the face and say I do not love you? What would you think of me then?"

" I should think what I think now, that your true heart had revealed itself to me in all honour."

" But I ought to know; it is weak to hesitate. I cannot bear to think that I may be deceiving you."

" You cannot deceive me. Let your heart be quite at rest, Do not question yourself and be troubled any longer, for, whatever comes, you will not have deceived me for one moment. But, dear, I think you will love me. Do you forgive me for feeling so sure?"

" Mr. Ogden, will I seem foolish if I ask you, how do I know but some day I may experience a stronger, deeper love than that which I feel for you? I have not seen everybody."

Philip smiled at her unconscious admission, and at the utter simplicity of her manner.

" Dear, you will honour me beyond all the world,

if you will give me the happiness of assuming that
risk." Then he said more gravely, " I know well
that I am no hero. You will meet many a person
more like the ideal man you may have dreamed
of loving, but I love you with my whole soul,
Leigh."

" When you speak so, you place me in a different
atmosphere. It is as if I were quite promised to
you," Leigh said, in a pained, low voice. " I have
always been so decided in everything, and I have
felt so distressed in the last few days, because of
my doubts. Love, real love, never hesitates so.
Are you sure that you understand ? I cannot feel
that I wish to lose you utterly ; yet, Mr. Ogden,
you are very far from being all the world to me.
Do you think you understand ? "

" Everything, everything, and what you tell me
makes me profoundly happy, and I love you a
thousand times more for every noble word you
have said to-night. I have unspeakable faith in
your perfect truth towards me. Whatever you do
will be sweet and right."

" I shall feel differently now. You are so good
it rests me."

" You have given me much happiness, such
blessed hope ! "

" Ah, but please do not be happy quite yet ! I
do not know."

" I know," said Philip, under his breath. " Will
you say good-bye to your sister and Tom for me ?
I want you all alone just as you stand there, so
fair and sweet, with the lovely eyes looking up at
me, and telling me that you love me a little, for

the very last picture I take away in my heart from here." And, bending again over the hands he held so closely, he said, "I am quite patient, only trust me, dear." And in a moment his step sounded rapidly on the pavement, and Leigh was alone. But not long was she left to her sweet meditations. Out came Tom, carefully guarded by Bessie. His long-suppressed mischief, forbidden to express itself in words, found vent in prolonged, inquiring stares, and glances of commiseration, and Bessie's most frantic efforts did not prevent him from drawling out, in a supernaturally solemn voice,—

" Blest is the tie that b-i-n-d-s
Dum di do, di dum de,
The fellowship of kindred m-i-n-d-s,
Dum di do, di dum de,"

as he passed Leigh her candle, and gave her an affectionate good-night.

CHAPTER XVIII.

"Whence came ye, jolly Satyrs! Whence came ye,
So many, and so many, and such glee?"
KEATS.

"WHAT amazing sounds!" exclaimed Leigh, as she, with Tom and Bessie, returning from Gem's, late one afternoon, rode slowly along the winding wood-road. "Are we coming upon sylvan deities at their revels?" And they all peered curiously through the trees.

The approaching sounds grew more distinct, and Tom remarked, "Whatever they may be, they are singing college-songs, with immense gusto ; and no faun that ever capered could shout in Blake's *basso profundo,* which greets me now, if my ears do not deceive me."

He whipped up his horse in some excitement, and a sudden turn in the road disclosed three young men, walking arm in arm, smiling broadly upon the universe, and melodiously chanting the inspiring strains of Crambambuli, while one of them vigorously beat time with a long leafy branch. When he saw Tom, he wildly waved his *baton* high in the air, and rushed forward. Tom made a dashing leap over the wheel of the old wagon, and ejaculating, "That eye! Those nose! 'Tis he!" ran to meet him, and the two in a pathetic manner threw themselves into each other's outstretched arms, while the long branch gently and ridiculously swayed over their heads.

"Ladies, pardon our emotion," said Mr. Blake, approaching the wagon, and receiving laughing and cordial greetings from Bessie and Leigh, "but we only arrived an hour ago. We were in search of you. My joy at beholding Tom's beloved form was uncontrollable. Here's Morton, whom you know, but perhaps you did not know that he is suspected of writing poetry; and my young brother, whom you used to know before he shot up so marvellously. Infant, make your best bow to the ladies. The gallant crew of the Idlewild is reduced to these three gloomy and ancient mariners, upon whom I beg you will take pity."

"You do look sad, Mr. Blake," said Leigh, "and the voices of all of you gentlemen sounded full of an untold woe as you crept so wearily down the hill. Did you venture, may I ask, to come through the village so?" And she looked smilingly at young Blake.

"We did not sing till we got to the woods, and Dick had no branch to flourish, and that, I suppose, added to our imposing effect; still we rather flatter ourselves we made a sensation. We marched arm in arm straight from the yacht to your present domicile, inquiring our way, of course. The inhabitants rushed to the doors and windows, and 'the little dog laughed to see such sport '—"

"And here we are, suppliants before you," interrupted his brother. "We have left all the good comrades, with whom we started, at one place after another on the coast. Can you join us to-morrow, Mrs. Otis.

"O, thanks, but to-morrow is so very soon ! "

"Have pity on Morton. He has to read his odes to our dull ears."

"I'm not conscious of having perpetrated an ode since I've been on the Idlewild," remarked the latter gentleman ; "but the most prosaic individual, like our emaciated friend," putting his hand on Mr. Blake's stalwart shoulder,—" might have a soul above mackeral, and immortalize himself in verse, if you ladies would only grace the yacht with your presence."

"And Will here," went on Mr. Blake, " he's young. He writes the Log and makes our puns. That is, he makes the most and the worst. We've tried to humour the child and laugh, but there has been an awful gloom over the yacht of late, and we can laugh no more. You ladies have kind hearts. Will you not encourage the youth ? "

" If you will allow me to offer you some friendly advice," said Bessie to Will, "I would suggest that you resign your office of punster-in-chief before Mr. Otis goes on board. He would be a powerful rival. His puns, when he is much excited, are the worst in the world. No one can possibly surpass him."

Whereupon the boy responded, that if he were forced to resign the only position in which he could hope to distinguish himself, he should rely upon the constant society of the ladies as a consolation ; which sentiment was warmly applauded by his elders, and his brother encouragingly remarked,—

" Bravo, Infant ! Never did better than that at your age, myself."

So they chatted in the " merry green wood," the young men grouped about the wagon in which the two ladies were enthroned. Eloquently did the Blakes plead their cause. The trip they proposed was to Mount Desert, and they promised, wind and weather permitting, to bring the ladies home within a week. Bessie's reluctance to leave baby for such an age was overcome by Tom, who asserted himself manfully, and declared that the nurse was a tower of strength, and that the small atom of humanity would thrive equally well, in the healthful country air, whether its mamma presided each day over its sleeve-knots, or resigned that arduous toil for a week. And Leigh's disinclination to leave Gem quite yet was met with facetious remarks from Tom, and importunate prayers from the other young men.

" Where is the boy ? Show him to me," said Mr. Blake. " Be he alive or be he dead, I'll take him along with us, if he is the one impediment in Miss Doane's path to the Idlewild."

" I only wish you might take him," said Leigh. " The dear child would be so happy to go ; but it would not be safe. He only sits up an hour or two each day."

" Blake, as you value your happiness, don't think of taking him. He would be worse on board than the man who shot the Albatross. Miss Doane makes a kind of fetish of him, and has imbued my wife with the same idolatrous, superstitious folly. I have succeeded thus far in preserving that sturdy uprightness which my biographers will vie with each other in praising ; and you, Harry, I know, have sufficient manly independence to be proof against any of their fatuous wiles ; but Morton, as everybody is aware, is uncommonly susceptible, and Will is over-young, and we might see four prostrate forms on the deck of the Idlewild bending in blind adoration before that Holbrook phenomenon."

" He's jealous, Mr. Blake," said Leigh. " Gem is a charming child, and you shall all see him, for he is going home to make me a visit, and I do not think I shall ever let him go away from me again."

" Happy, thrice-happy Gem ! " said young Blake. " But do not destroy my peace of mind by taking him on the yacht. Miss Doane likes young people. At present I am, at least, the youngest of the party. Perhaps she will deign to notice me. If that Gem appears, I shall be nowhere." And the Infant, a long, lank youth of nineteen, whose tall form had not had time as yet to " fill out," and whose face was fresh in its colouring and bright with good-nature and fun, tried to look disconsolate, and failed signally. " I may not be a Gem, but why may I not be somebody's own sweet Will ? And won't somebody help me with the Log ? It's an awful bore ! Miss Leigh, you and I used to be good friends in the mud-pie days."

" I will help you, you poor, abused boy," said Leigh, laughing ; and if you will be good to Gem next winter, for he and I are sworn friends, you know, I will be very good to you on the yacht."

"O heavens ! Hear that demented girl. ' Love

o

me, love my Gem,' is her one thought.   I took a
peep at the boy myself, to-day, though I do not
usually encourage him by so much as a glance.
You should see him.   Thin ! thinner than the Infant here, and about a third as long.   Ogden, who
used to be a man of sense, is gone daft on the subject, too and he sent on somewhere for an easy-
chair, which is luxurious beyond description, and
the idol sits in it, with fruit and flowers and other
votive offerings all about, and the Arabian Nights
magnificently illustrated, and Robinson Crusoe, and
a pile of books as high as your head, on a table
that groans beneath their weight ; and I think I
detected Leigh burning incense the other day.   Is
it not pitiable ?"

"But where *is* Ogden ?   Is he with the wonderful boy ?   Where shall I find him ? "

"Where the breaking waves dash high on the
stern and rock-bound coast of Manhegan."

"And is he off there ?   I depended upon him.
Frailty, thy name is Ogden ! "

"I'm glad of it !" exclaimed Will, savagely.
"There are men enough on the yacht.   We've had
a surfeit of them ever since we started.   *I* can sur-
vive the absence of Mr. Ogden, and if you want to
go off, Mr. Morton, to ' some unsuspected isle in far-
off seas,' I'll try to bear it.   Tom, you don't count,
because you are married.   It's no matter about you."
And the audacious Infant smiled insignificantly and
placidly at Leigh.

"I'm like Miss Murdstone.   'Generally speaking, I don't like boys !' " retorted Mr. Morton.
"This youth being the brother of my host, I have

thus far refrained from dropping into Davy Jones's locker, but there are limits to my forbearance."

Meanwhile Tom and Mr. Blake were discussing Philip's disappearance, and the probabilities of finding him. Finally, when all the doubts of the ladies had been met and silenced, and all the arrangements for the trip perfected, the party went on towards the village, with young Blake, however, in the wagon with the ladies. Tom tramped along with his friends. The woods resounded with " Gaudeamus," and milkmaids in distant farmyards lifted their heads in wonder and affright to listen to the echoes awakened by the classic

" Hey down derry,
We'll drink and be merry,
In spite of Mahomet's law."

CHAPTER XIX.

"Till there was none of them but fain would be
Set in the ship, nor cared one man to stay
On the green earth for one more idle day."
WILLIAM MORRIS.

"For Shadwell never deviates into sense."
DRYDEN.

PON the deck of the Idlewild* sat the Infant with a ponderous tome. Beside him were Leigh holding his inkstand, and Bessie aiding the important work of writing the Log by her sympathy and valuable suggestions. Thus inspired, the young man wrote as follows :—

TUESDAY, August 30, 11 A. M.

Left Edgecomb at 9 1-2 A. M. Wind southwest, blowing fresh. Barometer out of order. We have on board, in addition to persons who have already received in these pages more honourable mention than they deserve, Mr. Tom Otis, Mrs. Otis, and Miss L. L. Doane.

---

* The author would express her indebtedness to the veritable Log of a veritable yacht Idlewild for certain items which will readily be recognized by persons who have had or may have the good fortune of sailing in that most charming of crafts, and of being entertained by ts courteous owners.

She will also remark, in this connection, that while Edgecomb bears a slight resemblance to a pleasant old town in Maine in respect of its scenery, there the resemblance ceases. She therefore begs not to be accused of libel, and pleads with Sairey Gamp,

"Which naming no names, no offence could be took.

Mr. Tom Otis is the hero of twenty-nine pitched battles. His bones are whitening on a dozen tented plains, and the blood he has shed is of the best of Virginia. Jovial, witty, and of a large and varied experience, the party is anticipating a vast amount of entertainment from him as soon as he recovers from the sea-sickness which he is momentarily expecting.

Mrs. Otis and Miss Doane being at the present moment seated on deck with the historiographer of the cruise, and looking over his shoulder as he writes, he naturally feels the blush of ingenuous youth mounting to his brow, and shrinks from the presumption of reducing to cold, dull words the sentiments which their dazzling beauty and indescribable charm of manner produce in his mind. Not wielding the pen of a Jenkins, he does not know how to describe their costumes. He can, however, testify that he has just seen Mrs. Otis take from her travelling-bag a small cube of some mysterious white substance. The historiographer in trepidation ventured to inquire its name and use. The reply was, "Why child, it's only magnesia. We expect to see friends at Mount Desert, and we have not the faintest idea of looking like frights if we can help it." Whereupon these lovely ladies calmly cover their fair faces with a chalky mask, bestowing a double amount of care upon the tips of their delicate noses, where, they remark, "sunburn is so extremely unbecoming." The historiographer, lost in wonder, awaits further revelations from these marvellous beings.

2 P. M.

The day is delightful. Passed the narrows at 11.45, the Ledges at 12.10, and the Indian at 12.30. Saluted him, and dipped our colours, the pilot informing us it is customary to do the venerable old fellow that honour. His outlines in the rock are faint and shadowy He looks forlorn, and as if he had better depart at once for the land of the setting sun in search of his brethren. Without wishing to destroy illusions cherished by persons who go down to the sea in ships, sailing upon this beautiful river, and who fondly believe in the Indian, we, Miss Doane and the Infant, do not hesitate to affirm, that we can discover very little Indian indeed in the ledge where his historic form is supposed to be imbedded ; furthermore, we boldly state that the eye of faith is required to see any Indian at all; that he might as well be called the cat, or the goose, or the porcupine ; that we have no respect for him whatever ; and if the owner of the yacht persists in giving him a salute on our return, we shall manifest our disapproval by standing in silent dignity, with our backs turned to that aboriginal object, and our eyes fastened upon the opposite shore.

Not wishing to lose a moment of this glorious air and scenery, we lunched at 1.30 on deck.

Made Hendrick's Head Light at 2.30, and anchored in Cape Newaggen Harbour at 3.45. Tried fishing for a while before dinner, which was served at 5 P.M. Sun shining clearly ; air warm. Whole party a little fatigued with hauling up their lines to look at the bait.

The scene on deck during the evening was picturesque in the extreme. The ladies half reclining upon huge piles of cushions, fell into a dangerously sentimental mood. They dreamily remarked upon the beauty of the quiet little harbour, and the pretty outline of the shore. They were heard to express a fervent desire to

> " Eat the lotus of the Nile.
> And drink the poppies of Cathay."

Mr. Otis informed them that there was not a lotus or a poppy on board, and appealed to Blake, Senior, for corroboration, which was heartily given,—the latter gentleman remarking he would have ordered some

down with the last supplies, if he'd known the ladies
would wish that sort of thing. He volunteered to
send the steward in a small boat to the nearest place
on the coast where there was a druggist, for some mor-
phine, which did not sound so euphonious as "the
poppies of Cathay," but he presumed it would answer
the same purpose. The ladies objected to the flippant
style of conversation in which these two world-hardened
men indulged, and begged them to drink in the quiet
loveliness of the night, or at least to assume a virtue,
if they had it not, and be silent ; and soon nothing
was heard but the occasional breaking of the waves
on the great rocks that lined the harbour's entrance.

Inspired by the perfections of the night and the
beautiful Miss Doane, challenged by that wretched
pair, Otis and Blake, Senior, and strongly urged to
prove his powers by the ladies and the Infant, Mr.
Richard Morton distinguished himself by the following

"IMPROMPTU.

"O, the sea, the beautiful sea !
The earth and the sky are nothing to me.
Only the rise and the fall of the tide
Seem fittest to speak of with thee by my side.
For when thou dost smile, my hope like the flow
Of the incoming tide ever onward doth go ;
But when for the smile you give me a frown,
Like the outgoing tide my hope floweth down.
Then smile, and not frown, and close by my side
Let's float on the waves of the inflowing tide."

The historiographer does not know whether this is
or is not a very superior article, but inserts it in the Log
to help fill up, and because it is the best thing of the sort
that can be produced at present upon the Idlewild, no
man on board but Morton knowing how to mount any
kind of a Pegasus. The historiographer privately sus-
pects that Mr. Morton's 'winged steed' can't fly, and
that he is a gaunt, raw-boned nag,—a sort of Rosi-
nante.

The impromptu was received with great favour by the ladies, who declared that the beauty of it was, that Mr. Morton did not mean a word he said; in return they recited some charming poems. The writer of this chronicle, though young and inexperienced, as has been previously remarked, could but observe the striking earnestness with which Miss Laura Leigh Doane repeated, "Tides," a very tender and sweet love-poem by "H. H.;" and the intense feeling which she threw into the closing words, "Love has a tide!" almost made the innocent youth's hair stand on end with amazement. He happens to know that Miss Doane has been making the journey of life but two short months longer than himself, and he wonders how it is that she seems to have gotten such leagues in advance. He was about to propound this question in all sincerity, when a voice disturbed the hush that followed the poem.

"Leigh, that was very touching—very touching indeed. Harry and I wept to hear you go on in that style, but you were looking exactly in the wrong direction. Manhegan is over this way."

The meaning of which pleasantry, though half hidden, Morton and his historiograper dimly guess at, and long to sink the wretched isle and all whom it shelters beneath the waves of the Atlantic.

It is the painful duty of the Infant, as an honest chronicler of this cruise, to state that his brother, to whom he was wont to look for admonition, counsel, and example, and Mr. Tom Otis, a man for whom he has ever cherished the most profound veneration, did unite, deliberately, wickedly, and maliciously, to destroy the glamour of poetry and sentiment which all things else conspired to throw over the minds of the other members of the party. Morton and the historiographer were prepared to follow blindly where the ladies would lead, and they, though perfectly aware that they were safely anchored in the snug little harbour of Cape Newaggen, did not hesitate, as they listened to the ripple of the water against the yacht, to give utterance to vague and delicious fancies about " drifting along with the stream," and gondolas, and Venice, and "the magic of the sea ;" and they·recited many poems, and sung sweet songs in a way that was bewitching in the extreme to their two devoted slaves, but which led to deplorable results. The historiographer blushes to recall the scene that followed, and the heartless Vandalism of Messrs. Otis and Blake. They retired to the bow and held a whispered consultation, then returned, and Mr. Otis, in a grave and dignified manner, remarked that he was aware that they had not seemed entirely in sympathy with their surroundings, or with the refined and elevated sentiments of the rest of the party ; that it was not, however, always best to judge from appearances ; that their hearts were in reality profoundly moved, and in evidence of their sincerity they would beg to be allowed to contribute to the general happiness by reciting some poetry.

Here Mr. Blake remarked that he and Mr. Otis had most carefully observed the character of the poems quoted by the ladies, by their gifted friend, Morton, and by the young and promising Infant, and that they would not presume to introduce any inharmonious subjects. They would only venture to repeat lines relat-ing to the fathomless sea, or suggestive of longings after the unattainable, the might-have-been, the never-more.

Whereupon he formally stated that he now had the honour of presenting to the intelligent audience before him the popular reader and elocutionist, Mr. Tom Otis.

Mr. Otis gracefully bowed, and remarked that the title of the poem he was about to recite being sunk in oblivion, he would venture to call it, for reasons that no doubt a part of his audience would fully appreciate,

"A LEGEND OF MANHEGAN."

In a voice and manner that beggar description he began as follows :—

> " Poor Jonathan Snow
> Away did go,
> All on the ragin' mane,
> With other males,
> For to ketch whales,
> An' ne'er come back agane.

> " The winds bloo hi,
> The billers tost,
> All hands was lost ;
> An' he was one,
> A spritely lad
> Ni twenty-one."

Mr. Blake, when the excitement produced by his friend's recitation had died away, stated that it would be impossible to equal the pure pathos and graphic description of the fury of the elements, which he observed had electrified the listeners in the choice of Mr. Otis. Jonathan was a unique production, and stood alone upon the heights of literature. [Cries of Hear ! Hear ! from Mr. Otis, and groans from the ladies]. But the great heart of humanity can be touched in many ways. From the tender Folk Songs of a simple people, he would select some verses by an unknown poet—verses which contrasted strongly with the inspired vigour of the immortal Jonathan, but which in calm simplicity of diction, sweet regret, and patient sadness of theme were also unequalled.

"A DREAM.

> " I had a dream ;
> I dreamed I was alone,
> Alone !
> And oh ! it was so sad
> Away from home,
> From home !

"Upon the sand
  My eyes I bent,
                I bent !
  Upon my hand
  My head I leant,
        .   I leant !

"I thought of days
  Gone by and things,
                And things
  And simple
  Childish joys and string,
                And striugs !"

The ladies rose in disgust, and went below, declaring that men who ruin even the moonlight by such "horrid hideous notes of woe" ought to have weights and "things, and things," tied to their necks and be dropped into the sea.

It is suspected that the effect produced by these two designing villains was precisely what they had planned, the hour being 12 P.M., at which time dull, prosaic souls are apt to get sleepy. So ended the memorable evening at Cape Newaggen.

CHAPTER XX.

" End things must, end howsoe'er they may.'
                                                    BROWNING.

FRIDAY, August 31.

BEAUTIFUL weather. Left Cape Newaggen at 9 A.M., and went out to a fishing-ground for cod. The ladies appeared fresh and bright at breakfast, and Mr. Otis enlivened the party by making the astounding discovery that we have on board the world-renowned, graceless trio, Tom, Dick and Harry, associating intimately with an " L. L. D."

11 A.M.

Morton has just caught a forty-five pound cod, and is in a gloriously exultant state. He suggests that we unite in singing, as a morning hymn, the exquisite lines of Watts,—

> " Up from the deep
> Ye codlins, creep,
> And wag your tails about."

Passed Manhegan at 12 M. Whitehead at 2.05. P.M., and anchored at Owl's Head Harbour at 3.30 P.M., having had fine weather and a most agreeable sail. Off Manhegan an animated discussion was held. Mr. Philip Ogden—who, as he might have been on the Idlewild, and is not, is supposed to be labouring under a temporary aberration of mind, wandering about among the benighted peasantry of that island—was the subject of the debate. The question was finally voted upon : Shall the Idléwild put into Manhegan, and shall its dauntless crew seize the recreant Ogden *vi et armis?*

Ayes,—Otis and Blake, Senior.

Noes (loud and deep),—the ladies, Morton, and Blake, Junior.

The Noes were triumphant, Manhegan Light left in the distance.

During the afternoon of this day, fired by an unholy desire to wage war upon the finny denizens of the deep, and too finical to remove the article from his finger, to which it had an affinity, Mr. Tom Otis, in detaching a sculpin—a fish to which he was exceedingly partial— from his hook, threw into the raging sea a ring of considerable intrinsic and incalculable sentimental value. For further particulars inquire of Mrs. Otis.

He desired it to be distinctly understood, that he did not thereby wed the billows of Owl's Head Harbour. That they were not the Adriatic, and that he was not a Dog[e] that he should do this thing. It is suggested that, backed by the authority of the Arabian Nights, he shall offer a vast reward for the ring, and publically give notice that all cooks, stewards, and seafaring men shall hereafter exercise the utmost care in cleansing fish, lest they lose the opportunity of finding that one which wears now a precious jewel in his head.

Coming up on deck after dinner, a sudden silence fell upon our merry party, even Otis and Blake, Senior, being subdued by the magnificence of the sunset.

The Camden Hills to the northwest, Ragged Mountain and Megunticook, cold and in shadow, stood out in bold contrast against the brilliant warm sky. Silently we watched the golden glory deepen, and the wonderful rosy light that followed, and shone on the gleaming white sails of twenty or thirty little coasters lying at anchor around us, and that crept higher and higher, until its radiance was reflected in the water below, and the whole landscape was glorified. The last rays fell upon the bluff on which the lighthouse stands, and while the after-glow still lingered with its firy opal hues gradually fading away in deep violet clouds, we took a short sail out of the harbour, passing between numerous little rocky islands and reefs, gray-looking and cold, with the foam rising high around them, and miles in the distance was a huge fog-bank which seemed to be rolling in finely, but which did not once overtake us.

SATURDAY, September 1.

From Owl's Head to Eggemoggin Reach. Under weigh at 7 A.M., having secured the services of a new pilot, an ancient mariner remarkable for his misfortune by sea and by land. According to his own account, he had been wrecked on nearly every rock, cape, island and sand-bar from Cape Sable to the Florida Keys, and he certainly ought to know all the perils of our cruise. While sailing slowly up Penobscot Bay, with light breezes and fine weather, this old Jonah entertained us with an account of his experience in the law. He seems to have been always at law, and in fact had a case coming on when he joined us, and was in a continual fright lest he should not be at home in season for it. As he always got ashore in his voyages, so he was always swindled in his bargains. and seems usually to have gotten the worst of his lawsuits. The effect upon his mind was unfortunate. He entertained a special dislike for the legal profession, besides being generally misanthropic. His anathemas against lawyers met with the strongest encouragement and sympathy from those brethren in the law, and in all manner of mischief, Messrs. Otis and Blake, Senior.

Under his guidance we were lazily wafted up Penobscot Bay, with light northerly winds. Sailed through the Thoroughfare, and saw the great white dome of the

Isle au Haut, eight or ten miles to the south-east as we came up by North Haven toward Eagle Island Light, which, by the way, had the honour of gaining expressions of unqualified admiration from Miss Doane, and it will probably, on that account, hold its haughty head higher than ever above the waves.

A number of the islands were extremely pretty, as we sailed up the bay. We made Pumpkin Island Light at about half an hour before sunset, and anchored close under Little Deer Island, in Eggemoggin Reach. Miss Doane takes exceptions to the name of Pumpkin Island. Mrs. Otis also denounces it bitterly. They say that all the names have been pretty, Newaggen, Manhegan, Owl's Head, and Isle au Haut, and they also graciously approve of even Eggemoggin, Indian names, however unpronounceable, being always charming; but no words can express their contempt and loathing for poor Pumpkin Island. Mr. Otis remarked that he presumed Asphodel Light House or Fringed Gentian Islet would be more likely to find favour with the sickly, morbid fancy of certain persons he could mention, but that for his part he admired Pumpkin Island hugely. It was a good, substantial, sensible, honest name, and patriotic, moreover, as it commemmorated the national dish of New England—pumpkin pie—and he wished he had some.

The Infant records this speech, not because he regards it as in the least amusing or instructive, but merely as an illustration of the heartless, he might say sinister style of comment in which Mr. Otis and Mr. Harry Blake have taken incredible delight during the whole voyage.

SUNDAY, September 2.

Passed a quiet day at anchor here, not because we were afraid we would be drowned and made into a tract to frighten small boys if we should continue our course on Sunday, but because the ladies say the Reach is too lovely to leave. It is like a great, calm, broad river, and the mainland opposite to us has a well-cultivated look, and the soft green of the turf and foliage is pleasant to look upon.

Those ungodly men, Otis and Blake, Senior, took the small boat and went off to the ledge with guns They returned with three coots, and were not recognized by the respectable members of the party. We sent them to Coventry for the remainder of the day.

MONDAY, September 3.

Know all men by these presents, that I, being duly sworn, do testify, that, in the judgment of the whole company on board the Idlewild, Monday the third day of September, 18—, Mr. Tom Otis did then and there eat, beside the regular courses, at dinner, of soup, meats, and vegetables—,

> Fifteen olives,
> One box of sardines,
> Eight sandwiches,
> Two cocoanut-pies,
> Five loaves of cake,
> A bottle of chow-chow, and
> Seven cups of coffee;

and for so doing was awarded the first prize, having distanced all competitors.

(Signed) CHARLES WILLIAM BLAKE.

Witnesses :
BESSIE D. OTIS.
LAURA LEIGH DOANE.
RICHARD HENRY MORTON.

Blake, Senior, being host, feels that courtesy forbids him to testify.

Passed out of Eggemoggin Reach, the fertile look of the country vanishing, and the bleak, wild, out-at-sea aspect increasing more and more as we left the large Deer Isle and sailed among numerous white, ledgy, islands, and soon approached the promontory of Bass Head, the southern point of Mount Desert. We sailed past it, into Southwest Harbour for the superb view, and saw the Mount Desert Hills rising grandly before us, while Some's Sound, that wonderfully pretty sheet of water, its calm clear blue contrasting with the "tumultuous sea" outside—"the rough green plain that no man reaps,"—ran, straight and narrow, far into the island between bold, high cliffs, like a Norwegian fiord, we who have never seen a fiord confidently assert.

Passed between the Cranberry Islands and Bear Island Light.

Made Bar Harbour at 5 P. M., and were speedily visited by troops of friends. The historiographer would gracefully excuse himself from a description of the magnificent scenery of Mount Desert. For information which he has the discretion to omit, he would refer future perusers of this Log to artists known to fame and many authors of repute.

He is aware that he has omitted to mention various points of interest along this attractive Maine coast, and he would say, in apology, that but nineteen summers have passed over his head, and that he has been too much interested in playing piquet with Miss. Doane, to tear him away from that charming amusement, and devote himself to the dreary labour of making nautical and geographical observations.

The voyage has been all sunshine and gladness.

We do not design to exhibit the swiftness of our craft, as the sailing powers of the Idlewild have long since been proven, but have wished merely to sail here and there at the will of our fair passengers. That our return voyage may be as happy, is our devout hope.

In conclusion, it may be well to mention that there has been an entire immunity from sea-sickness, although Mr. Richard Morton dined one day upon deck, making an entire repast upon one lemon.

P

The Idlewild party is now strolling about on the rocks in a state of perfect bliss, all except the poor historiographer, whom an inhuman brother has left behind to complete the Log, and do the honours of the yacht to such visitors as may appear.

The Idlewild people were received with great rejoicing by numerous friends at Bar Harbour, and it occurred to one hospitable soul to give a pic-nic of gigantic proportions to their honour. The guests, sixty in number, were bidden to the feast at seven o'clock, and shortly after that hour the bluff over Anemone Cave was the scene of much hilarity, as gay groups of friends ate sandwiches, drank coffee, and gossiped, with the grand old ocean rolling in solemnly below them.

"Leigh," whispered Tom, "don't drop your muffin on the buttered side, or pour your coffee down your sleeve in your agitation, but Ogden came over to Southwest Harbour yesterday, and he arrived here to-day, and he's about five feet off, just behind you, and he's coming this way as fast as he can, but somebody—an uncommonly attractive young lady, by the way—has just buttonholed him. I did not tell you all at once, for fear you could not bear it."

In a moment Philip approached, and saw Leigh's

> "Sweet face in the sunset light
> Upraised and glorified."

And though the "madding crowd" was there and the senseless chatter, and the commonplace bread and butter and pickles, the inexpressible gladness in her eyes, as she turned and looked up at him, told him that his brief absence had been a sagacious thing, and that the pearl was his own. He wondered if the voluble young lady on the other side of him ever would cease urging him to partake of the salad over which she presided, and if picnics at Bar Harbour went on forever. The two talked nonsense with the others, and ate they knew not what.

At last the darkness deepened. The moon rose superbly over the sea, and everybody climbed down the rocks to the shore to see what wonders were going on in the Cave.

Into its mysterious depths two gentlemen had vanished. Presently its recesses were illumined by a gleaming red light which disclosed its little shining pools of water, and its rough jagged sides, and shone out upon the groups of ladies and attendant cavaliers at different heights on the cliff, and met the moonlight far out on the waves with a singular effect. A yellow light followed, and a ghastly green, and then these wizards of Anemone Cave sent off some rockets, and various other whizzing things.

"I do feel really disappointed," exclaimed Bessie. "I always had a profound respect for a rocket. I thought it quite a magnificent spectacle; but doesn't it seem small, and mean, and insignificant, and frightfully impertinent, for it to go buzzing away at the old ocean?" Receiving no reply from Philip and Leigh, to whom her remark was addressed, the kindly disposed little woman went on, "O dear, dear! I actually believe there is my Tom flirting with Miss McArthur. She's entirely too pretty, and she knows how! Where *is* Mr. Morton? O Mr. Morton, would you be so kind as to take me round to the other side of the cliff? There's something going on there which I must put a stop to at once. Would you believe it? that incorrigible husband of mine—"

She vanished, and Leigh and Philip wandered away over the rocks.

An hour later they sat together, caring little for the vast cliffs towering above them, or for the foaming surf at their feet. They saw but the gladness in each other's eyes. Their own murmurs spoke a mightier language in their ears than the voice of the great waves. Yet they sought in vain to express the meaning that overcharged their hearts, for

> " Love's tenderest, truest secret lingers,
> Ever in its depths untold,"

and its sweetest words are only

> " Like sighings of illimitable forests,
> 'And waves of an unfathomable sea."

*   *   *   *   *

" And are you glad to see me, dear? And are you quite 'sure of yourself' now? And is it like your 'theories?'"

" I was very, very glad, but I think you took an unfair advantage in surprising me, and some day I will have my revenge."

" And will you go out on the prairies and live in a log-cabin with me, if ever I ask you? Will you, Leigh?"

" No, sir, never, if you persist in remembering
all the idle words I ever said, and wickedly repeating them to me."

" But would you, Leigh ? " he persisted.

" I am really disappointed in you already. I
never dreamed you would develop into a tease like
Tom. Do you know, I've read that success ruins
some natures ? "

" But would you ? "

She hesitated ; then, " I will go to the very end
of the world with you one day if you should wish,"
she said in low earnest tones. " Why do you make
me tell you ? You know so well."

" Forgive me Leigh ; it is so sweet to hear you
say it, how could I help asking ? But, dear, if
ever I ask you to live in a log cabin, it shall be
only for a couple of months in the summer. And
the cabin shall be as pretty as you please, and it
must be at Edgecomb somewhere. How would our
island do, just where the old fort is ? "

" And it must be called ' The Gem,' " said Leigh,
amused. Then, realizing that this was indeed giving to remote and shadowy things a " local habita-
tion and a name," she sprung up with a sweet shy-
ness in her face.

" Shall we not find Bessie now ? "

Suddenly she stepped back to Philip. The moon
shone gloriously on the water, and threw its white
radiance over the girl as she said impulsively,—

" Please sit down, just where you were. There
is something I must do. Close your eyes," she
commanded. Philip obeyed. Half tenderly, half
laughingly, she murmured, " This is reparation."

And he felt the light, timid touch of her lips on either closed eyelid. "I am so sorry,—I was so sorry then,—I have been sorry all the time," she murmured. "How cruel I was!"

And Philip, with his great happiness sounding in his voice, yet with the same lightness of manner which Leigh had assumed, to cover a strange depth of emotion, said,—

"That memorable blow did close my eyes for a time, it is true, but only to open them to new and wonderful radiance. My whole life shall show you my gratitude for it. Think to what honour it has raised me. My darling, my queen, it was my royal accolade."

THE END.

Toronto: Printed by Hunter, Rose & Co.

www.ingramcontent.com/pod-product-compliance
Lightning Source LLC
Chambersburg PA
CBHW030808020726
47499CB00006B/1822